The Princess of Convenient Plot Devices

1

Mamecyoro

Illustration by
Mitsuya Fuji

YEN ON
New York

The Princess of Convenient Plot Devices

1

Mamecyoro

Illustration by Mitsuya Fuji

Translation by Sarah Henshaw

This book is a work of fiction. Names, characters, places, and incidents are the product of the author's imagination or are used fictitiously. Any resemblance to actual events, locales, or persons, living or dead, is coincidental.

WATASHI WA GOTSUGO SHUGI NA KAIKETSU TANTO NO OJO DEARU Vol.1
©Mamecyoro 2017
First published in Japan in 2017 by KADOKAWA CORPORATION, Tokyo.
English translation rights arranged with KADOKAWA CORPORATION, Tokyo through TUTTLE-MORI AGENCY, INC., Tokyo.

English translation © 2022 by Yen Press, LLC

Yen Press, LLC supports the right to free expression and the value of copyright. The purpose of copyright is to encourage writers and artists to produce the creative works that enrich our culture.

The scanning, uploading, and distribution of this book without permission is a theft of the author's intellectual property. If you would like permission to use material from the book (other than for review purposes), please contact the publisher. Thank you for your support of the author's rights.

Yen On
150 West 30th Street, 19th Floor
New York, NY 10001

Visit us at yenpress.com
facebook.com/yenpress
twitter.com/yenpress
yenpress.tumblr.com
instagram.com/yenpress

First Yen On Edition: December 2022
Edited by Yen On Editorial: Leilah Labossiere, Ivan Liang
Designed by Yen Press Design: Andy Swist

Yen On is an imprint of Yen Press, LLC.
The Yen On name and logo are trademarks of Yen Press, LLC.

The publisher is not responsible for websites (or their content) that are not owned by the publisher.

ISBNs: 978-1-9753-5283-7 (paperback)
978-1-9753-5284-4 (ebook)

10 9 8 7 6 5 4 3 2 1

LSC-C

Printed in the United States of America

Library of Congress Cataloging-in-Publication Data

Names: Mamecyoro, author. | Fuji, Mitsuya, illustrator. | Henshaw, Sarah (Translator), translator.
Title: The Princess of Convenient Plot Devices / Mamecyoro ; illustration by Mitsuya Fuji ; translation by Sarah Henshaw.
Other titles: Watashi wa gotsugou shugi na kaiketsu tantou no oujo dearu. English
Description: First Yen On edition. | New York, NY : Yen On, 2022–
Identifiers: LCCN 2022037172 | ISBN 9781975352837 (v. 1 ; trade paperback) | ISBN 9781975352851 (v. 2 ; trade paperback) | ISBN 9781975352875 (v. 3 ; trade paperback)
Subjects: CYAC: Fantasy. | Reincarnation—Fiction. | Characters in literature—Fiction. | Brothers and sisters—Fiction. | Gay people—Fiction. |
LCGFT: Fantasy fiction. | Gay fiction. | Light novels.
Classification: LCC PZ7.1.M359 Op 2022 | DDC [Fic]—dc23
LC record available at https://lccn.loc.gov/2022037172

The Princess of Convenient Plot Devices

Sirius

The crown prince of Esfia and the soon-to-be king. A handsome, intelligent, superhuman top.

Sil Burks

The main character of the BL novel *The Noble King* and Sirius's boyfriend.

Enoch

The current king. Since he's married to a man, he and Octavia are not blood-related.

Alexis

Esfia's second prince. Octavia's confidant and beloved little brother.

Meet the characters of *The Princess of Convenient Plot Devices.*

Klifford Alderton

Octavia's bodyguard. His past seems shrouded in mystery…?!

Octavia

A former high schooler who was reincarnated into the world of *The Noble King*. She's the princess of Esfia and a *fujoshi*—a fan of man-on-man romance novels.

1

Oh, if only this story were about someone else.

If only I were my former self, alone in an empty classroom, witnessing this scene as an innocent third party. Then I could have just reveled in the passionate flames of Boys Love fangirldom.

But alas. Now that I'm a participant, the flames of my little *fujoshi* heart now burn eons away.

Oh, wouldn't it be nice if I had playfully sneaked out to the castle town to catch a glimpse of guilty bliss between two men I didn't know? Even in my current incarnation, my heart could have still burned on.

Why'd it have to be...my brother...?

I frowned. A man-on-man love scene was unfolding before my very eyes. And not in 2D but 3D. They were both extremely handsome. Both of them were locked in a world where only the other existed...and their tongues were locked, too.

And who were they? Well, one of them was my big brother—sad but true. And the crown prince, at that. As in, the soon-to-be king.

We were in a corner of our majestic and splendid castle, the pride of Esfia. The tactful among us automatically avoided this area so as not to disturb my brother and his lover, but this space was actually meant to have people coming and going all the time. It was a hallway. And not a hallway reserved for the royal family but a hallway that could be used by castle servants or guests, so long as they had permission.

I suspected funny business was afoot...

Ordinarily, there would be more people around, but there was not even a single maid or guard present.

And now I know why—my brother is in the middle of a tryst!

I loudly snapped the fan in my hand closed. And in a hallway where the only thing you could hear was the naughty sounds of the lovers exchanging saliva, that was more than enough to procure the desired effect. The boys' lips parted with a start.

"Octavia...," said my brother when he registered my presence.

"Dear Brother, it pleases me that you and Lord Sil get along so well. However, we must be considerate when choosing the locations of our rendezvous."

Don't make out in the hallway, assholes!

Oh, I wish I could have said that part out loud! But my brother is a prince, and I'm a princess. I must sugarcoat my speech in a manner befitting my royal status.

I am Octavia, the eldest princess of Esfia. I'm sixteen years old, and my brother is nineteen.

My brother, Crown Prince Sirius, furrowed his brow.

God dammit! You're so frickin' hot!

Silvery hair, aquamarine eyes, tall, handsome, intelligent, and gifted in martial arts—he's a total superhuman. It's no wonder that in my past life, I fangirled *hard* for him—and it's no wonder the fans ranked him at number one. We do love a top!

"Forgive me...," my brother apologized in what was, incidentally, a voice so sexy it could make you swoon.

"No matter," I answered...then there was silence.

Well, this is awkward...

Oh, and look at my brother's boyfriend, Lord Sil. He feels just as awkward as I do. Oh, and now my brother's squeezing his hand supportively. Aw, they're sooo in love.

Encouraged by Sirius's support, Lord Sil turned to me. "Princess Octavia."

Lord Sil is an androgynous hottie. He doesn't look like a girl, but he is beautiful. He and my brother make a beautiful couple...of boys. The son of a baron, his relationship with my brother came to fruition after many twists and turns.

And he's also the main character.

"What is it, my lord?" I asked, cool as a cucumber.

The solemn look in Lord Sil's eyes tugged at my heartstrings. But even though I'm a former degenerate *fujoshi*, I'm a princess now, and I've spent years cultivating my impudent facade.

"Princess Octavia...what must I do to receive your approval?"

"Approval...is not mine to give or to withhold. Who do you take me for? I fully understand that you are the man my brother loves, Lord Sil. Is that not enough?"

Lord Sil winced in sadness.

In *The Noble King*, Octavia was the biggest supporter of Sil and Sirius's romance.

But...I am not that Octavia.

2

In my past life, I was a *fujoshi*—that is, I was a teen girl who was an avid consumer of man-on-man romance media.

My favorite novel series at the time was a unique work from a publisher with a primarily female audience. It was a Boys Love fantasy series set in another world called *The Noble King*. It's no exaggeration to say that this series defined my three years of high school. While most high school girls came of age reveling in 3D, my 2D *The Noble King* and I were inseparable.

Its popularity was boosted with a spinoff manga series, then drama CDs, games, and anime, growing it into an expansive franchise. Oh, I spent every last yen of my high school allowance on it! Those were the days...

But my favorite incarnation of the series had to be the OG novels. Sil, who was born under suspicious circumstances to a baron, had a fated encounter with Sirius, the crown prince of Esfia. They fell in love and had to overcome many obstacles together. The end.

Well, technically, I died before the story actually ended.

In my past life, I was Maki Tazawa. I died when I was sixteen. And the cause of my death was... Well, I do remember it, but I'm redacting it. It brings back all sorts of bad memories, so I usually keep it locked away.

Anyway, I died, and then I was reborn.

Actually...I was supposed to be reborn into a much crueler world, but according to my bad memories, luckily (though that's up for debate) I escaped that fate and was reborn into the world of *The Noble King*, the series Maki Tazawa so dearly loved...

...as the main character's boyfriend's little sister.

Little sister...or *Sister-dearest*. In my past life, that's what I used to call Sirius's younger sister: Sister-dearest. Whatever the medium, the treatment of female characters in the Boys Love, or BL, genre was often a delicate issue. They were either villains who tried to separate the hero from his love interest, or they were the lovers' confidants.

But in either case, girls were always side characters. So how were girls treated in *The Noble King*, you may ask?

It was the latter!

From the very first volume of *The Noble King*, Octavia, the eldest princess of Esfia, was popular with the readers and a success story for BL female characters everywhere.

Octavia was a kind, understanding girl who loved her big brother. She was quite humble for a princess. And she was the ultimate ally for the two main characters: Lord Sil and Prince Sirius. Whenever the lovers were in crisis, her loyalty was unshakable—she even helped solve their inability to produce an heir. She was the epitome of a support character.

That's who Octavia was in the book series.

But this Octavia—me—was born with the consciousness and memories of my past life as Maki Tazawa and then raised as a princess in this world.

And...it kinda sucks.

It was a major disappointment. 'Cause you see, the point of the little sister in this BL series is to be a convenient resolution to the plot. Where we're at in the story so far, the issue still hasn't been brought up in the House of Lords yet. But if the story continues on its current course, the plot point in question will eventually come to pass.

Now, let me repeat, I am in a world modeled after a BL fantasy novel. My big brother is the crown prince and soon-to-be king. Obviously, this means he is a man.

The love of his life, Lord Sil, is also a man. But two men cannot possibly produce an heir together. And no, there's no miraculous plot twist, like, where one of the two boys was actually a girl raised as a boy all along.

And what's more, Esfia is a kingdom that observes strict monogamy—one woman for every man...or in my brother's case, one man. And here's the kicker: Even though this is a fantasy setting, there's no manmade drug or magic spell that can help two men make a baby together.

So whatever shall they do?

I mean, even in a BL world, surely there must be some practical way of sowing one's seed to create an all-important heir, right?

Well, here's the problem: This is a wholesome love story.

My big brother refuses to make love to anyone other than his true love. "Without love, I would never!" he says. "I could never do something so impure!" he says. "I could never betray and hurt my Lord Sil!"

That's how it went down in the novels, and judging by what I see in my brother and his lover now, it doesn't look like they'll veer off script.

If they were commoners, I doubt this would even be a problem. But my brother is royalty. The crown prince. The soon-to-be king. That comes with certain duties, you know?

And nobody's asking that they break up—he just needs to make a baby with a woman! That's the perspective those in his inner circle can't help but have. But my brother Sirius refuses. For true love, that is one thing he absolutely cannot do!

Back when I was Maki Tazawa, I remember hunching over the book at this part, raptly taking in every word! *Oh, Sil! You poor man! Oh, Sirius, I feel for you! I know he's royalty, I know he's gonna be the king, but c'mon, let him be faithful to his man! These two men are in love; just let them commit! Nooo, Sirius! Please don't screw a woman! Begone, evil bitch!*

The readers empathized with the leading couple and didn't want Sirius to cheat on his man, even if it was to create an heir. But if nothing was done, the royal family of Esfia was doomed. So narratively, how could one solve this problem?

I'll tell you how. Enter the dashing problem-solver of a little sister, Octavia.

"Fear not, dear Brother. When I bear a child, please raise it with Lord Sil as your own."

See how it was her idea? That's the beautiful part of it. She wasn't forced into it—she did it all of her own free will! Su-weeet!

The heir problem was a problem no more! Lord Sil and Sirius's love would prevail! And the readers all heaved a sigh of relief.

However...don't forget that *I* am Octavia now. You know what that means?

It means sometime in the future, I'll need to have an arranged marriage, give birth—more specifically, to both a boy and a girl—and give my children away to my brother.

The average age at which ladies of Esfia are expected to marry, regardless of class, is twenty, give or take three to four years. Which means I'm about at that age. And even though I am a princess, I wasn't betrothed to anyone at birth or anything like that. Apparently, this is so I can be married off to the most beneficial husband for the sake of the kingdom.

If you dig deeper into the royal family history, there were some marriages that were love matches...but there weren't many. Most marriages like this were arranged, and at the very least, the princess must give birth to one boy and one girl.

A boy to be the next in line to the throne, and a girl to give birth to the next heir after him. If I give birth to a third child, I'd finally get to keep it and raise it as my own.

So that's basically how it works.

When I read the story from Sil's perspective, I never realized any of this—it wasn't until I became Octavia that I learned of the dark side to BL novels!

Throughout the generations, Esfia's crown prince would fall in love with a man (and not want to do it with anyone other than him), so his sister would get married (oh yeah, this applied to previous generations, too!) and give birth... Rinse and repeat.

And now that I'm the one this is happening to...it really sucks.

I hate this shit!

Complaining is all I have left, really. It's like, don't I have any freedom? What if I were a lesbian or something?!

But you see...I really can't do anything about it. And even if I could, my best chance would still be to give up on romance and have an arranged marriage to a man.

You read that right. I mean, I'm stuck in a BL novel. This world favors man-on-man romances. And as Sister-dearest, I am merely a convenient plot device to preserve the way this world works.

In other words, I exist so that this story's main character can marry Prince Sirius—another man—be allowed to love him faithfully, and to give the happy couple an heir and children to raise as their own and live happily ever after.

And in my former life, I was a fangirl whose heart burned hard for their love story. I was like, *Good thing Sister-dearest was there to take care of the heir issue, huh? All's well that ends well. Love rules!*

But now that I *am* Sister-dearest...

Um, dear Brother? You're the crown prince and soon-to-be king. So even though your marriage to a man is kind of set in stone—make your own damn baby!

That's where I'm at.

Now that I'm Sister-dearest, I know just how heavy the burden of solving the heir problem really is!

Lately, a thought keeps coming to me: Palace harems and polygamy are actually pretty nice. In my former life, I was absolutely against cheating, and the idea of polygamous harems generally made me feel sick.

But in a system where the king was placed at the top, as long as the man was a satisfactory stud, don't you think a harem would actually be a pretty good system for solving the matter of an heir? You know, since it fulfills his obligation to bear children.

In that regard, harems are fabulous. Totes fabulous. Esfia should definitely add a royal harem to the royal castle!

Anyway... Being reincarnated into my favorite novel series, *The Noble King*, was nice and all, but I'm really bummed that I was cast as Sister-dearest. So, naturally, I don't have very positive feelings for my big brother.

Don't get me wrong, I do love him as the top who hooks up with the main character. But looking at this from Octavia's perspective...I just can't like him. In fact, I often snap at him without meaning to, and I'm a far cry from the kind, understanding princess I'm supposed to be in this story.

Even though I was born as Octavia, I still have Maki's memories in my consciousness. In the book, my big brother and I were inseparable, but now...we're not even all that close.

I just can't help but be uncomfortable with Octavia's role in the novels. Then again, my future has yet to play out. With parts of my future still unknown, through trial and error, my relationship with my brother has settled into what it is now.

As for Sister-dearest's best feature—her humility—well, honestly... not sure I've got that, either. It's an established fact that Sister-dearest is polite to those beneath her. And I'm *probably* like that. In a world where I'm in the upper crust, I mustn't completely ignore the responsibilities that come with it...

Yeah, sorry, that was a lie.

I mean, I'm a princess—of course I'm gonna take advantage of the power I have! That's the way I've lived my life!

At any rate, having a bad relationship with my big brother was enough to make some enemies. Which resulted in bullying! From men, no less! I know they say women fight dirty, but it turns out hell do hath fury like a woman scorned—and it's *men*!

So you know what I did? I used my princess privilege to banish those bastards to faraway lands! It felt so frickin' good, too! Privilege rocks.

Sooo, in short, my personality is a far cry from the devoted younger sister in the OG books. And so is my position—my once harmonious relationship with my big brother is now pretty rocky. Flimsy, even.

But on the surface, we act as though everything is fine. We're a loving family. Neither my big brother nor his followers have ever harassed me even once...and it's a damn shame.

If my big brother had a rotten personality, then I'd have some justification! But my brother Sirius is a perfect superhuman, whose only weakness is Sil.

And this Sirius is just as he was in the novel: fully devoted to his lover. He's not the sort of guy I could convince to make love to some chick to solve the heir problem. Though if he were like that, I'd change my tune and bend over backward to support him!

After all, there are many women out there who would gladly help my big brother conceive an heir. I'm sure some of them would do it just for the seed of the crown prince alone, and some would set aside their personal feelings and volunteer as tribute to preserve the delicate balance of power among the nobles in court—he'd have his pick of the lot.

But I doubt my brother would agree to that. Because he loves Lord Sil.

So honorable... Oh yes, he is a very virtuous man! I get it, he's noble. And if I weren't caught in the middle of this as Octavia, or if my brother weren't the next in line to the throne, I'd have nothing but good feelings about him!

Romance between two men (as long as it doesn't directly affect me) is still one of my favorite things! I love that my big brother and Lord Sil are in love! They're still my BL OTP, my absolute favorite one true pairing—that hasn't changed.

I went through a phase where I wished they hadn't met…but then I realized my brother probably would've just gotten together with some other guy instead, which made me grateful that it was Lord Sil.

But I was still facing a roadblock: the heir issue. And since my brother and Lord Sil had left that problem unresolved (and passed the buck onto me), I have a hard time liking them.

Even the sturdy princess facade I'd cultivated was slipping, and my true feelings were threatening to come out. I couldn't hide my feelings from my brother and Sil forever.

My brother wanted his sister's blessing. And Sil wanted his partner's family's blessing. It's only natural that they'd seek it out.

My brother aside, it's obvious to me that Lord Sil is sick with worry about it. Because even if I pretend not to notice, everyone else in the castle won't shut up about it!

Even my father, the current king of Esfia, and the (male) mother who raised me have welcomed my brother's romance with Sil with open arms. And as a result, try as I might to hide them, my sore feelings just stick out like a sore thumb.

3

There I was, standing in the hallway where I'd just witnessed my brother and his boyfriend having a tryst. After reflecting on my situation as a princess, I tilted the tip of my closed fan against my forehead and sighed.

My future...it looks so bleak!

Hey, you'd want to go all melodramatic heroine, too. Though I'm technically not the heroine... In the world of BL, I'm just a side character!

Then the air stirred, and a certain someone stepped in front of Lord Sil. "You...you say you will never give us your blessing?"

Whoa there! Big Brother has muscled into the conversation!

My brother always got uptight when it came to the love of his life. Though, since he was a perfect model of a man by nature, his devotees adored this more human side of him.

My blessing... My blessing, eh?

Well, they were certainly blessed in the looks department. Their hotness just tickled my *fujoshi* heart to death.

The only reason I had such a negative bias toward them as a couple was because of the heir problem, nothing else. If only I could be sure my brother would bear his own child in the future.

Maybe I should just ask him right now?

After all, at present, the only reason I am so sure of the future is *because* I have knowledge of what happened in the books. But that was just my speculation. It wasn't set in stone.

Also, I'd never had a deep conversation like this with Sirius before because our relationship was so delicate. I didn't even have an in! But luckily, now that I had both my brother and Lord Sil together, I could ask them their opinion on the matter.

I also wanted to know how Lord Sil felt about it. In the novels, Sister-dearest and Lord Sil were on speaking terms. But me? Well, my brother feels pretty protective of Lord Sil, so I've never been able to get him alone.

"Dear Brother, you and Lord Sil intend to marry, no?"

That's how everything had been written. The make-out scene I'd just witnessed was either born of marriage jitters or was a sneak attack to jump Lord Sil. They were usually all over each other in the court. So he wanted to spice things up a little and strengthen their bond with some surprise nookie.

"Yes. I do," my brother answered without hesitation.

"But you two are both men," I said, firing the first shot. "How do you intend to produce an heir?"

The color drained from Lord Sil's face. Meanwhile, my brother glared at me.

Y-you don't scare me, okay?! I opened my fan and shut out my brother's eyes. *Nothing penetrates my death ray shield!*

"Are you suggesting that I seek out a woman for marriage?"

"Whether you marry her or not is of no concern to me. I am merely considering the matter of your child. Lord Sil is incapable of giving birth, is he not? And yes, Lord Sil...I wish to hear your thoughts on the matter as well."

"W-well, I...think..."

Well, well, well. So it seems like even the overly optimistic Sil has at least given some thought to kids. But I guess his heart just hasn't caught up with his head yet.

Ohhh... My burning fangirl feelings from my past life are coming back to me! Oh, Lord Sil! You poor, sweet boy! I know! I know how you feel! Please believe me when I say I don't hate you for this at all! If anything, it's the opposite!

"The one I love is Sil, no other," Sirius declared.

Thank you, dear Brother. I was about to be swayed by Lord Sil, but now you've snapped me back to my senses!

How! Ever! That isn't exactly the issue here! You know it isn't, and you're avoiding it, aren't you?

"You would never understand; you don't love anyone."

......

Speech...less. I was stunned speechless.

So this was what it felt like to boil with rage. Setting aside that Sirius was happily in love with Lord Sil and had his head in the clouds...of all the things to say...

I don't love anyone? He meant romantically, right? That I don't have a boyfriend. Well, of course I don't? Neither as Maki nor as Octavia have I ever loved anyone deeply.

When I was Maki, I went to an all-girls school, not coed. I was pretty preoccupied with *The Noble King* anyway, and I thought I still had my whole life ahead of me, so I didn't bother with 3D romances.

Which is why things are different now that I've been reincarnated!

This time around, I want to marry someone I love. But Octavia was only a convenient plot device, and this is a BL world besides, and, real talk, the only romance happening around here is man-on-man! Heterosexual couples are the minority in these parts! My first love here as Octavia was my personal bodyguard, but he wound up hooking up with a man, too! I mean, even if I did fall in love with someone, and even if the feeling were mutual, I wouldn't be allowed to marry him unless it was beneficial for the kingdom, because I'm frickin' Octavia!

I felt something snap inside of me.

"Oh, but I do have a beloved."

"What?" my brother asked. *You've never mentioned him before,* his eyes added.

Well, of course I never mentioned him before. Because he doesn't exist! It was a bald-faced lie! I was caught in the moment!

However... Being caught up in the moment can yield terrifying results at times. And the moment I was caught in refused to let me go.

"Why, yes. And I shall introduce my beloved to you and Lord Sil quite soon."

Before I realized it, I was running my mouth. I scare myself sometimes.

Shut up. You don't have a beloved. You don't even know any guys who would play along and pretend to be your boyfriend. You're in deep shit now.

Should I just apologize and say it was all a lie? Apologize? To my big brother?

"You would never understand; you don't love anyone." His words immediately invaded my brain.

Over my dead body!

"Well, good afternoon." I smiled, elegantly walking away.

I'm gonna find a decent man if it kills me! I vowed firmly in my heart.

* * *

Luckily, I'd said they would meet him "soon." Just vague enough that I still had time.

I had a few days…and if I avoided my brother like the plague, I could probably buy myself a whole month.

A man… A man! I know a place where I can come and go freely and that's also full of men!

I wandered quite a bit away from the hallway where my brother and Sil were. I turned and looked behind me.

"We're going to the training grounds."

"Yes, Princess," my bodyguard answered with a bow.

He had been in my shadow all this time, even when I'd had that interaction with my brother and his boyfriend. He always masked his presence, so it really was like he wasn't even there. Sometimes I even forgot I was being guarded!

Since I was a princess, it was regulation for me to always have a bodyguard in my company, even inside the castle walls. And the bodyguards of royalty were always handsome and intelligent. But I cycled through them rather quickly.

And why was that, you may ask? Because these bodyguards would always fall in love with some guy and move away! And a princess's bodyguard was particularly vulnerable to this, since his work hours were long.

As Octavia…my first love was one of my bodyguards. His name was Gray. I still remember him, even after all this time. He was kind, strong, handsome—I mean, could you blame me for falling for him?

But my first love tragically withered away. I guess you could call that my true initiation into the BL world.

And where was my first love now, you may ask?

Gray hooked up with his childhood friend, the son of a baron! He was adopted into their family by marriage, and he now lives in that baron's domain as its lord! The end.

In this world—mostly in my own kingdom of Esfia—same-sex love and same-sex marriage (usually an adoption by marriage, except for royals, who have actual marriages) were not at all unusual among the upper class. It was, in fact, quite common among most families in the aristocracy. If anything, commoners were more likely to do the opposite. Among the commonfolk, heterosexual marriages were the norm, whereas homosexual marriages were not so common.

And as you might have guessed, everyone in my circle is of the aristocracy! Therefore, man-on-man romances are the golden standard.

As a princess, my main romantic targets were my bodyguards, since they were closest to me, but ever since Gray, every bodyguard assigned to me would always fall for another man, then either quit or transfer away and live happily ever after...

But did I learn my lesson? Nope. Time after time, I fell for my guards. It's happened to me five times now, with Gray at the top of the list... so it's definitely been a learning experience.

Bodyguards? Those heartbreakers are a no go! A lady must *never* consider them romantic targets!

Ohhh, I want you by my side forever, brave knight, uwu—nope, you won't see a dash of that from this girl!

Now I see bodyguards as entities who are assigned to me, then after a short while, they're replaced. I don't even bother to learn their names.

Then again...hasn't this one been with me for a while now?

I glanced over at my current bodyguard. He was glancing back at me, which meant our eyes wound up locking.

Short black hair hung softly down to the top of his collar. His eyes were a deep indigo. His nose was handsome. His face was chiseled and nicely proportioned. He was tall, and given that he was a knight, the muscles under his armor were surely toned.

Yeah...he's a hottie, all right. God dammit. But I'm sure this guy is destined to wind up with some hot ikemen or pretty-boy bishounen.

I was sure of it...but...

Huh?

I was secretly perplexed. On second glance, I couldn't help but find him confusing.

This knight... I thought he was the son of a baron or something.

And since the eldest son of a noble always took over as head of house, he had no business becoming a knight without a good reason. Which meant he was either the second- or third-born son. And he was in his early twenties.

But most of all, just look at him. He's a fine specimen. An excellent specimen, even. So I'd just assumed that he would fall in love with some other guy and leave right away, but he's been with me how long now... three months? I've lost bodyguards in as little as one week... Wait, no, it was three days! I set a new record for the changing of the guard at the beginning of this year...

Up until now, it seemed like there was a direct correlation between hotness and the length of a bodyguard's employment. The hotter the bodyguard, the faster he'd hook up with another guy and quit...which begged the question...

"Hey, you..."

Maybe I might as well ask his name?

"Yes, Your Highness? Is something the matter?" His clear, deep voice resounded.

Aha. That's a no.

I shook my head. *Yep. Called it. This guy's a no-no. Hot face, hot voice—he's the whole package! Any day now, he's bound to hook up with a suitable guy and move far away! Asking for his name is a waste of breath.*

"No... Never mind."

"......"

"......"

Urgh. Great. After months of barely talking to the guy, you had to make it awkward by being like, "Hey, you..." out of nowhere! I'd better say something...

"Be sure to keep me guarded at all times," I commanded blandly, using my position as princess to cover my ass.

"As you command, Your Highness," he answered with a little bow.

"Yes, very good."

Very good! Now we're back to normal princess-bodyguard dynamics!

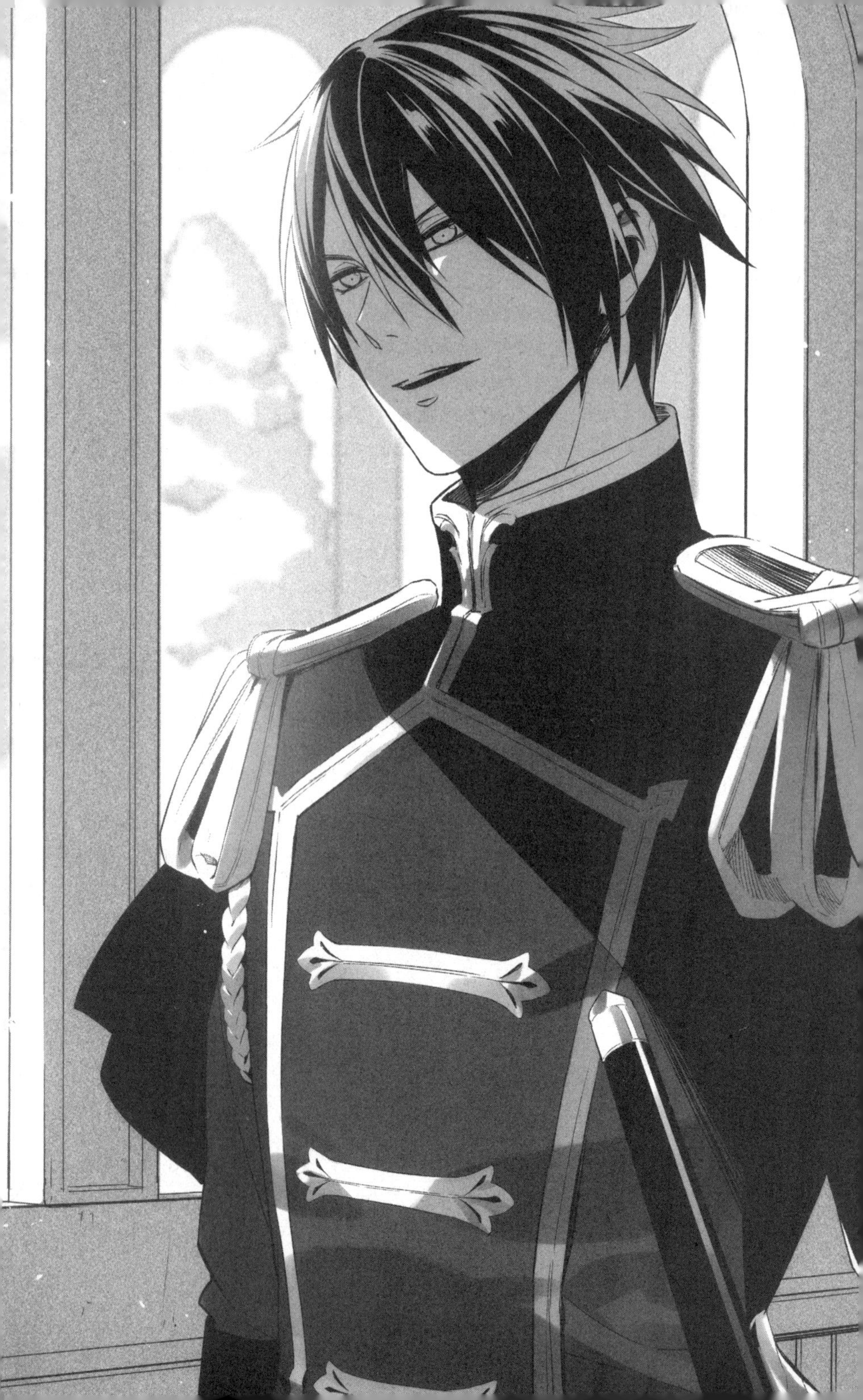

I regained my composure and resumed walking toward the training grounds.

There, I'll find a wide variety of men! Soldiers will be there! And...lots of them will be paired off with each other, but still!

Geez, isn't there a gentleman I can convince to play my boyfriend lying around somewhere? I don't care if he's highborn or lowborn—so long as I can use my princess privilege to exploit him!

4

At long last, we arrived at the training grounds! Though they were only practicing, the fighting sure looked realistic. My little brother and a soldier were sparring with swords.

Why, yes, I also had a little brother, two years younger than me. A pretty boy whose golden hair and bright emerald-green eyes could blind a person—a real bishounen.

My little brother was also a character in *The Noble King*. He was there to serve as occasional opposition to his big brother, Sirius. He wasn't really mentioned much in the OG novels, so I didn't really know what kind of relationship he had with Octavia there, but to me, Alexis was my best friend. I even called him Alec for short—that's how close we were.

Incidentally, my family was composed of a father (the king of Esfia), my adoptive mother (a man, who was a former merchant and a commoner), my big brother, Sirius (birthed by our father's elder sister—our aunt, who died right after childbirth), me (birthed by my father's younger sister—my other aunt), and my little brother (born of a duke's daughter and our father after a mistaken night of drunken passion).

You could call us siblings...but we were all technically cousins, I guess.

And what's more, even though nobody ever said it aloud, there was this stinging sensation that, when it came down to the bloodline, wouldn't the younger brother actually be the heir to the throne—not the eldest son?

He even looked the most like Father.

But regardless of blood, on paper, we were all siblings. And unlike our elder brother, who lost his mother the day he was born, Alec and I both were taken from our birth mothers—even though they were still living—and raised apart from them. I would only ever see my birth mother once every few years.

It wasn't until right after I turned fifteen that I was given the freedom to see my birth mother whenever I wanted. I imagine it was because younger children would be more likely to take a preference to their birth mother... But it wasn't because I couldn't call my adoptive (male) mother "Mommyyyy!" and have him dote on me. It was the sweet smell and soft body. When I was little, I longed for her to hold me more. If I hadn't had my memories as Maki to fall back on, I probably would've gone full rebel.

But I still had it good—I got to see my birth mother, after all.

My little brother wasn't so lucky. His birth mother, the daughter of a duke, was quietly whisked away to another land, married off, and was currently living a modest life...a life where she's not allowed to leave home.

As for the motive behind the misdeed that night, she claimed herself that she had become overcome with lust for my father...but I didn't quite buy it. That's because she already had a boyfriend, who was now, apparently, her husband. What's more, her husband was a gardener and very lowborn. Real talk, noble-born girls were political bargaining chips. They were always married off to the most suitable men.

Adultery was a fatal scandal to an unmarried woman, which was exactly why she did it—she consented to the scandal to make the impossible possible. Anyway, the whole thing reeked.

The fact that she got pregnant on the first try only further fomented my theory.

You see, there was a potion that helped a woman get pregnant on the first try. If a woman took the potion and laid with a man, she would conceive on the spot. However, she would suffer extreme health complications—the worst of which would be losing her life.

Additionally, it was unlikely she would be able to conceive another child. That's why nobody ever used the potion unless they were desperate. It was difficult to obtain, too. It was that kind of sketchy potion.

And how did I know so much about the aforementioned potion, you may ask? Why, because everyone in my sphere kept suggesting that—worst-case scenario—I might have to use it myself someday! Yup! It was apparently a secret reserved exclusively for the nobility!

Hence, Alec's birth mother. My theory was that she had used that potion, but that got swept under the rug. Actually, the fact that it got covered up was, in itself, pretty sus.

Anyway, my father was furious at the time. I'd heard he'd wanted to punish her severely for it, but it was kind of like, for what crime?

For assaulting the king? Sexually? That definitely would be a crime.

But all she really did was serve him wine—at the very least, she didn't drug him. That information was widely accepted. She had no intention of harming the king.

So if you had to name her crime, I guess it would be "Making love and getting pregnant."

And I mean, this is gonna sound crass, but I was honestly shocked to hear that my father was actually capable of making love to a woman! Like, even if you're drunk, you'd totally notice. Saying he mistook her for the (male) love of his life was a real cringey excuse! Like, think of the body mechanics!

Actually, I think the majority of the duke's family were on Team Duke's Daughter. It's not like everyone was on board with the fact that the king married a man and couldn't bear his own children.

That's why she was sentenced to a life of seclusion in the tiny domain owned by her father. She was never to return to high society again. And her son—my little brother—was taken from her, and all her rights as mother were revoked.

Because of this, my little brother has never once met his birth mother.

What's more, according to my father's train of logic, my little brother was a mistake. A stain on love. But in blood, he was the rightful heir.

This whole scandal was sometimes a major source of stress for me. I mean, my baby brother was a shining star! Yet his family treated him with…well, not with hostility, but the air was always a little tense.

My father believed the duke's daughter had conspired against him, and our adoptive (male) mother saw Alexis as the true blood heir that he was unable to give his beloved husband. And since Sirius loved his father and adoptive (male) mother very much, he empathized with them, and while he wasn't cruel to our little brother, he did keep Alexis at a polite distance.

As for me, I love my birth mother to death. And since I never really felt close to my father or adoptive (male) mother, I wound up interacting a lot more with my little brother. You could say it was inevitable.

So that's why my little brother and I were super tight.

Alec was fourteen years old. And he was sure to become an excellent specimen in the future. If I had my way, I'd love for him to marry a pretty girl someday…but I don't think that's gonna happen.

Not in this world—this BL world, you know?

I mean, I'd be cool with Alec marrying a cute boy, too, of course. But man…it would sure make my burden a little lighter if my little brother would make a baby, you know? Y'know what…

"Dear Sister! How unusual to see you at the training grounds." My little brother stopped his sparring session and rushed over to see me.

My face melted into a smile. "Yes, well, I had a little matter to attend to…" *I'm on a manhunt, baby!*

"What little matter?" he asked in a dubious whisper, looking behind me…at my bodyguard.

Oh?

Usually, my bodyguard kept watch over me from a slight distance, but he was very close to me for a change.

Oh, is it because we're at the training grounds? Yeah, even though it's still technically inside the castle walls, we are out in the open. I guess it makes sense to change positions accordingly.

"He isn't masking his presence today, I see," Alexis murmured to me with a questioning glance at my bodyguard.

"Indeed." I nodded to put him at ease.

But...is he right? Does he actually have a presence right now?

Sometimes I think to myself, *Ooh, it feels like I'm walking all by myself! He doesn't get in the way at all!* (And to be fair, I have a feeling the main reason for that is because my bodyguard never says a word on his own.) So I'd always talk about my bodyguard like, "*He masks his aura perfectly! It's like he's a wisp of air!*" But that was just an expression. Just an expression!

That's right. For me, invisible things like auras or bloodthirst—unless I can see them with my own eyes, they might as well not exist. All I'm able to perceive is how physically close or far away another person is from me.

But someone like Alec who can detect auras? Now, you'd be crazy to call someone like *him* normal.

"Comparatively speaking...it seems he's been your bodyguard longer than most," Alec said.

"Yes, it's true," I confirmed, nodding sincerely.

I hear that. I'm a princess! Why do they keep changing on me so fast? But wait?

Alec—my baby brother—was staring intensely at my bodyguard.

Hey. Why the bedroom eyes?! Huh? Wait a minute...

D-don't tell me...my baby brother was hit with Cupid's arrow? Oh, God, Alec...not you, too! Oh...I'm so sorry! But there's just no way I can be supportive of your romance right now! I know I was just thinking that I'd be cool with my baby brother marrying a guy, and I know I predicted my current bodyguard was bound to leave me soon, but if he left me for Alec? Talk about major psychological damage...!

"Oh, no you don't, Alec. He's my bodyguard." *Let's nip this in the bud, shall we?*

"Well, now you are being even more uncharacteristic," Alec said. "I've never heard you speak up for a guard so. You there. Tell me your name."

Eep! His name? Why does Alec have to ask my bodyguard for his name? This can only be an expression of interest!

But...wait just a second now...

My bodyguard showed no sign of answering. I turned around to find the knight standing still as stone behind me.

"Hey. You," Alec prompted him again.

But there was still no answer. *Well, this is certainly awkward.*

"You. Answer Alec at once," I commanded him.

And with a little bow, my bodyguard finally spoke. "My deepest apologies. But, Princess Octavia." He paused, his deep blue eyes focused on mine. "The one I serve is you. Without your express permission, I cannot answer anyone, not even your brother. If anyone asks my name, all the more so."

"My, such dedication...," I said with a smirk.

Come to think of it...if someone asked a subordinate his name and he answered of his own volition, that basically meant "Consider this my letter of resignation." A changing of the master, so to speak. But what it would really be considered was a betrayal.

And actually, I'd compleeetely forgotten about that! But stay with me here!

This was a custom that dates way, way, waaay back into Esfia's history. Now, if both parties were well aware of the meaning behind it, it was a rather significant act, but that practice was a shell of itself now. It had scarcely crossed my mind up until now. But I did see this custom come up in Volume 5 of *The Noble King*, when Lord Sil used it to get a new subordinate.

Alec smiled suddenly. "You refuse to speak directly to me because I am not your master. Are you suggesting that I ask my sister if I wish to know your name? My, you are quite the old-fashioned one."

It seemed that Alec understood.

Whoa, would you listen to that sass?! My Alec is growing up, and I don't know whether to be proud or sad about it. Between that and the recent growth spurt, I'm starting to see glimpses of a rebellious phase, dear Alec. But your princelike mannerisms are on point!

Completely unlike me. Even though I was born a princess, my past life as Maki made it a real struggle to get my speech and mannerisms up to par for a royal! It's like, since I already had the worldview and feelings of a modern-day Japanese girl as my foundation, it was hard to get my bearing right.

"Dear Sister," Alec said, returning his gaze to me. I guess this was his special way of asking me to tell him the name of my bodyguard.

In other words, I have to tell Alec the name of my bodyguard right now. But, um, Alec? As much as your dear sister would love to tell you his name…I don't know it, either, buddy!

It sucked, but if I just told Alec, "*I dunno!*" he was sure to be disappointed in me. I hid my face behind my open fan.

I hope he didn't see how shifty my eyes were… Wait, Mr. Bodyguard! Good sir, is that a twinkle in your eye behind that wooden facade? Are you mocking me? Wait, do you know that I can't answer?

Aha! Just got an idea.

I closed my fan and pointed its tip at my bodyguard. "I, your master, am giving my express permission. Tell Alec your name."

This just might work!

"As you command, Your Highness," my bodyguard answered reverently, going along with my scheme. "I am Klifford Alderton."

According to my knowledge from my past life as an otaku, or diehard fan, most court names in European settings originated from the domain a person came from. And in the world of *The Noble King*, the nobility in my own kingdom of Esfia used their surnames as their court names, so it's all very easy to remember. There weren't any deathly embarrassing situations where you'd be like, "*I know I'm the Duke of A, but my name is B, not A!*" or you'd ask someone's surname and you'd be like, "*Oh, so you're Duke Somethingoranother, right?*" only find out that he's actually a viscount and has a different domain name! Nope, none of those misunderstandings here!

I know this sounds weird coming from me, but I'm not really all that bright. I sucked at math and at English. I may have an extra sixteen years' worth of memories, but that's it, really. And I'm not sure if my sixteen years as Octavia added much to that... I get the feeling they didn't.

From the moment I was born, I had memories of my past life. This meant I was a very precocious child, and many people fawned over what a genius I was, but the closer I got to the age I died at in my past life, the less praise I received. And now, I act my age. This was my true mental age all along.

But let's put a pin in that...

So my bodyguard is a son of a count from House Alderton, eh? The Aldertons made a name for themselves among the nobility as a military family. Wait...huh? But I thought they only had daughters. Were there any ikemen of marriageable age in that family?

Alderton... Alderton... Hmm...

"Klifford Alderton, you say?" Alec asked.

Hmm? C'mon, Alec, why're you all surprised?

"Ridiculous. Why is a bastard like you my sister's bodyg—?"

"Alec. You shouldn't speak like that."

Alec, I've never heard you curse before!

"But, Sister!"

"Her Highness permitted it," my bodyguard, Alderton, interjected. His eyes were locked right on me.

"No... Sister, is this true?" Alec asked me, his eyes filled with bewilderment.

What Sir Alderton was saying here was that he, Klifford—well, I don't suppose his first name mattered here, but his family name might come in handy in high society if he ever were to stop being my bodyguard—got permission to be my bodyguard from me, right?

I searched my memory. Three months ago...Alderton's predecessor had a fated encounter and ran off with his beloved after a mere three days. He was a real overachiever, that one. So I needed to find a successor as soon as possible. Then, a few days later, my chief lady-in-waiting gathered up some candidates and brought them to me for approval. And I think Alderton was among them... Yeah, probably.

And when it came time to make my decision, I used a special technique from my past life. I did eeny-meeny-miny-moe. I mean, no matter who I chose, he was just gonna up and leave anyway. Why be selective, right?

So anyway, the name my finger landed on wound up being Alderton. So I had handed the paper to my chief lady-in-waiting, told her I chose him, and called it a day.

And the very next day, Alderton became my bodyguard.

Then, fast-forward three months. My days were peaceful, and Alderton was loyally carrying out his duties.

I smiled at Alec. "Why, yes. I chose Alderton myself. And he is serving me very well."

"Dear Sister..." Alec sighed. "...If you say so, then it may not be my place to complain. But still..."

Alec sulked, his father's golden hair hanging in his eyes. I reached out to him instinctively.

"Sister...what is it?"

Unable to resist the temptation, I tousled his hair. When we were younger, I'd tousle it mercilessly without a second thought, but now, perhaps due to his rebellious phase, whenever I'd touch his head, Alec wouldn't reject me outright, but he would look a bit grumpy. But that made him even more adorable!

I removed my hand from his head and squeezed him in a tight hug.

"Agh! S-Sister!"

"Oh, Alexis, I love you so much." Then I gave his head a couple pats. This was my self-care!

Alec sighed heavily in my arms. "Sister...you should try having your own head petted."

He wants to...give me head-pats?

"Oh my. Are you going to pet my head, Alec? Very well... I'm waiting." I hunched over slightly.

Alec slowly reached out to me. He rested his hand on my head, then rubbed. He stroked my head a few times before lowering his hand and

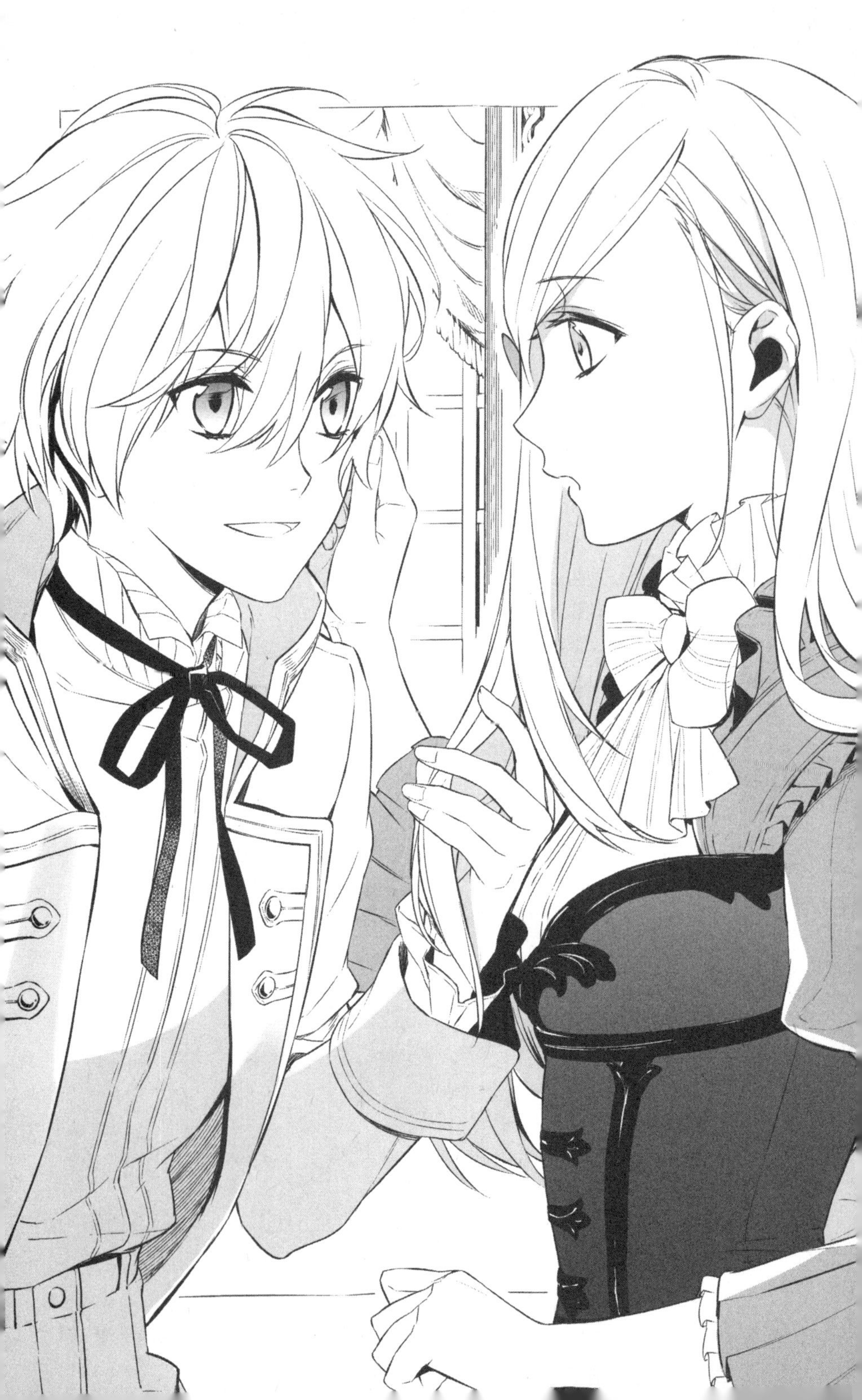

lifting my loose tresses in his fingers. Thanks to the diligent work from my handmaids, my hair was silky as a shampoo commercial model—it's my pride and joy!

"Sister...I could get used to this."

"Oh? But my hair is not as fine as yours, Alec."

"Oh, no, Sister. Your hair is definitely superior."

"You think so? Perhaps you see me through rose-colored glasses? Any other man would—"

"Don't tell me you intend to let another man play with your hair." Alec pulled my hair. It hurt.

"Oh, Alec. You know full well there is no other gentleman in my life who would caress my hair. It was merely conjecture."

While Alec was technically a man, he was my baby brother, so he was the one exception. And if there were such a man in my life, I would've gone straight to him to be my pretend boyfriend...

That's right! I'd gotten so caught up in my little soothing head-pats from Alec that I'd completely forgotten. I came to the training grounds to hunt for a man!

I hastily gave the training grounds a once-over. But...all it did was discourage me.

Hey, soldiers over there holding hands, what's with the shy giggling and lack of personal space? Damn honeymooners!

Hey, instructor and student over there! What, am I supposed to believe that you're hugging him from behind just to teach him how to swing a sword?!

The training ground was full of hot guys...just like I knew it'd be.

But this won't do... Oh, the happy auras of the male couples are stabbing my heart with all kinds of mixed feelings...

The *fujoshi* half of my heart was shivering with unadulterated fangirl bliss, but the single-girl half of my heart was hit with the harsh reality that there was no room for me... It sucked.

This is bad... Now, just the sight of the young soldier who was sparring with Alec earlier walking over to a corner of the training grounds and talking with a fellow soldier made me think they were a couple.

"Alec…"

"Sister?"

"Please…stay by my side for a while longer." *I know he'll have to leave the nest someday! Please let it be in the distant future!*

Alec smiled sweetly at me. "Of course I'll stay, Sister."

My baby brother is an angel!

The Overanalyzed Career of an Ambitious Common Soldier

One day, the princess of our kingdom set foot on the training grounds.

Her little brother, Second Prince Alexis, was quick to react. The moment he saw her, his eyes immediately lit up, and he said, "I'm going to say hi to my sister. Take a break until I return."

No sooner did the words leave his mouth than he left my side, running. These abrupt changes in his demeanor always made me doubt my eyes. And who could blame me, given the way Prince Alexis usually acted?

I was a new recruit, chosen from what were likely many candidates to assist the second prince with his sword practice. And when I noticed a good portion of the other soldiers were glaring at me, clearly with jealousy born of lovesickness, I gave up and withdrew.

Despicable... Look, guys, your creepy behavior is the very reason why Prince Alexis didn't choose you!

As I walked away, I happened upon a fellow soldier who was also on break, so I decided to kill time by shooting the breeze with him for a while.

Still, my eyes couldn't help but wander over to the royal siblings.

There was Octavia, the first princess. At sixteen years of age, she was just the sort of princess commoners such as myself had pictured back in my home village. She looked so different compared to the girls who lived where I came from. Silvery hair, aquamarine eyes, willowy and delicate—words like *pretty* or *girlish* described her face better than *beautiful*.

She looked very kind and gentle. She was the physical manifestation of a dream princess. At present, she was smiling sweetly at her little brother, Prince Alexis. As I watched him relax and smile with such ease around his sister, it was hard to believe he was so cool and curt with us soldiers.

And right beside the sibling sweethearts...

"Look at that handsome fellow... You know who he is, right?" the soldier with me murmured. "He's the same guy who was on the battlefield that day."

Hey, don't call him a "handsome fellow." You remind me of my ma back home.

My armored colleague was a commoner, just like myself. Commoners who wished to become soldiers had a harsh road ahead of them. We needed either connections, coin, or competency.

And if you had none of those things, your only choice was—strange as it sounds—committing some heroic act on the battlefield. Most commoners were used as cannon fodder and died...but if you managed to survive, you would be a hero.

My armored colleague and I had broken through the glass bulwark and become castle guards by the fourth method.

One year ago, when Saza Church crusaders waged war against the crown, we fought in the king's army. The Saza faith was the religion with the most followers in Esfia, but their defeat in this war brought to light a scandal the likes of which our kingdom had never seen before, causing their church to lose a lot of influence.

The biggest hit to the Saza followers was the assassination of their leader. That spelled victory for the crown, and it was a devastating blow to the Saza Church. However, for some mysterious reason, the king was currently seeking the man in charge of the assassination so that he could be punished.

Well, I'm sure there were some dirty politics at play between the Saza

Church and the crown, the likes of which commoners such as myself couldn't begin to imagine.

There was a man who fought in that battle...one called the Emissary of Ongarne. It's a name we made up. Nobody knows whose side he was on: the Saza Church or the crown. And that's because he killed soldiers on both sides.

Ongarne was the Saza followers' version of Hell. It was an abstract place of the utmost pain and suffering. And to mock the Saza scandal that erupted in conjunction with the war, one of the dominions was also named Ongarne.

Anyway, someone decided to call that man the Emissary of Ongarne. Meaning he was the one who escorted people to Hell. My armored colleague and I both had seen the Emissary of Ongarne on the battlefield.

And now, the spitting image of the Emissary of Ongarne—the one we saw on the battlefield that day—was on the opposite side of the training grounds, serving as Princess Octavia's bodyguard.

I nodded. "Yeah, it's really him."

"So...how much do you think Princess Octavia knows?"

How much does she know? That's a good question.

In the first place, it was only by mere chance that he and I even knew what the Emissary of Ongarne looked like. So we didn't doubt that he was an actual person of flesh and blood. But now that everyone was far from the that battle in both time and space, the Emissary of Ongarne became more and more of a legend with each passing day.

He was considered a fabrication created by many different people. Even in aristocratic circles, mentioning the Emissary of Ongarne would get you laughed out of the room.

So what did the royals think? The royal family consisted of His Majesty the King, His Majesty the Queen, Prince Sirius, Prince Alexis... and Princess Octavia. I found it hard to believe that the princess could truly claim to be ignorant.

Which meant...it was possible that someone had pulled some strings to get the Emissary of Ongarne to become the princess's personal guard.

It was seeming less and less likely that Princess Octavia was in the dark...

"Do you think she knows...and she's got him right where she wants him?" I asked my colleague. "You heard that rumor, right?"

There were whispers in the wind that the Saza Church leader's assassination was orchestrated by the Emissary of Ongarne. Whether you believed the Emissary of Ongarne existed or not, you had to acknowledge the crown's common interest there.

Princess Octavia was delicate—the perfect princess. But ever since I got posted at the castle, I started to hear rumors that there was more to her than met the eye.

If Princess Octavia knowingly welcomed a traitor into her arms, what was her reason...?

I vigorously shook my head. My armored colleague shivered in turn.

"N-now, now, let's not let our minds wander to strange places," he stammered. "There is such a thing as an uncanny resemblance. We might have both misremembered him, too."

"Y-yes, you're right," I said, choosing to go along with his declaration. It was technically possible that Princess Octavia's bodyguard just happened to bear an abnormally strong resemblance to the Emissary of Ongarne...not like I believed a word of that!

My colleague added, "And maybe he became Princess Octavia's bodyguard by some mistake!"

I couldn't help but interrupt in earnest, "But even if that were true... Princess Octavia herself has the final word on who becomes her bodyguards, right?"

"Oh...good point."

I blundered big-time. I steered the conversation back into foreboding territory. I need to talk about something lighthearted.

"Oh, that's right! Now, just think about it. If that villain really were her bodyguard, do you really think things would be this peaceful around here?"

The Emissary of Ongarne must have been Princess Octavia's bodyguard for a month now...or even longer? Yes, he has been here awhile.

I continued assertively, "Just look. Princess Octavia is surrounded by peace itself. Not an inkling of bloodshed. Not one suspicious death."

My colleague nodded firmly. "Hmm... True."

"As long as nothing's gone wrong, what's the harm?"

After all, at present, there was something besides the Emissary of Ongarne that posed a much greater threat to us.

"Yeah, I guess the Emissary of Ongarne isn't a real danger at the moment," my colleague agreed. "But...the biggest problem we're facing right now..."

"...Is the jealousy of other men," I said, finishing his sentence. We looked at each other and exchanged tired, understanding nods.

Our airing of grievances switched from the Emissary of Ongarne to the issue of factionalism among the guards.

It was...a matter of life and death.

This was our only chance at getting a leg up in life. We were given big farewell banquets when we left our villages to be stationed here. Returning home unemployed...would be social suicide. Our families would be happier if we'd died in battle and received gold as consolation. They'd no doubt erect some lovely memorials in our honor.

At this point, remaining a lowly foot soldier in the castle would be preferable to going home. Unless we raised our social standing somewhat, our wages would remain feeble. We could get married, but good luck feeding a family on our paltry earnings. A little cottage in the royal capital was a dream beyond a dream. We were doomed to a life in the barracks for eternity.

In order to escape such a gloomy future, there was just one problem with working your way up as a castle guard: where you were posted.

Where was the most advantageous spot for commoners like us to get ahead?

Most of the soldiers here were Prince Sirius's devotees. That man was overflowing with charisma, and he was gifted to boot.

But here's the problem...

My colleague and I were currently stationed in the unit directly reporting to the royals. We may have been nominally accepted into the ranks of the castle guards, but we were still in training. Once our training as new recruits was completed, as long as there were no exceptional grounds for denying our request, we would be allowed to work for whichever royal we wished.

And we were almost finished with our training. We had two choices: Prince Sirius or Prince Alexis. Princess Octavia was not an option. That was because as a lady, she was unlikely to have a great need for soldiers in battle.

So did we want to serve as a commander, or improve our social standing in the future and get recognition that way? In a way, those were our only two choices. And ordinarily, most common soldiers never got a chance to speak directly with either prince.

Both myself and my colleague did have opportunities to speak with Prince Alexis, and we often were his sparring partners, but we were rather rare exceptions. Since we had absolutely no pedigree, in addition to our way of thinking being a bit different from highborn soldiers, we were also well suited to Prince Alexis's personal circumstances.

"From a power standpoint, it's overwhelmingly Prince Sirius, right?" my colleague asked.

And he was right. Prince Sirius was next in line to take the throne, and he wasn't unkind to the common man.

"But Prince Sirius already has a fine collection of gifted subordinates. And they're all of noble blood and formidable in their own right," I said, calmly laying out the facts. They weren't all bark and no bite—they really were a gathering of incomparable men.

Between talented aristocrats and talented commoners...who had the advantage?

Now, here's another scenario: talented aristocrats and...average commoners. Who do you think's going to get the lucky break?

"Commoners like us just don't have a way to muscle into Prince Sirius's camp," my colleague grumbled.

I grumbled in turn, "I guess our only choice is Prince Alexis after all... If we work hard enough, we just might have a chance at climbing the ladder."

In the end, that was the conclusion we reached.

"You're right. And Prince Alexis is also no slouch himself. Plus, he doesn't seem to mind our company, even though we're commoners."

"Yeah...but..." I trailed off.

Prince Sirius didn't discriminate based on social standing. But Prince Alexis was a staunch classist. Most of the time, at least.

So why did he ask for us to be his training partners, when we were new recruits and commoners, besides? That was because actually, Prince Alexis had criteria he prioritized more than social status when it came to interacting with people...with men, that is.

I took a breath and finally spat it out. "Here's the problem... It's the way the aristocracy thinks, indulging in man-on-man romances without considering the consequences."

And then the bastards who get influenced by that—the soldiers who fall in love with Prince Alexis—assail us with acts of sabotage, harassment, and general jealousy!

Since Prince Sirius already had a lover, we wouldn't have to endure such things in his service. Which meant our problem was unique to Prince Alexis, who had no lover.

As if to pour salt into the wound, my colleague said something even more frightening. "More importantly...it's only a matter of time before we begin to follow that way of thinking."

"!"

I was trying not to let my mind go there, but he just had to go and say it!

He was right. There were soldiers among us who were noble-born and romantically attracted to men. They weren't rare, but they were outnumbered by commoners. And there were even a few soldiers who were lowborn but had climbed the ranks.

Among commoners, opposite-sex romances were the norm. But here in the royal capital...we'd become the minority!

And as for the soldiers from commoner backgrounds...those

lowborn soldiers, who had little experience resisting the allure of man-on-man action, would invariably, after enough time working at the castle... Well, most of them became very comfortable with (if not insistent on) doing it with men!

Because of this, our fellow lowborn comrades who had been stationed in the capital for some time would give us coy looks as if to say, *You boys are bound to join us one day...* Naturally, there was no such thing as lady soldiers in Esfia. All the soldiers were men!

The horror... The unbearable horror.

My body would not stop shaking. While it's inappropriate for me to say so, I understood how Prince Alexis felt. Though our stations in life, and everything else about us, could not be more different, we did have one thing in common: We only had eyes for women.

Prince Alexis's disdain for men was clear. It would be more accurate to say that he considered any man who had romantic feelings for him to be scum.

However, he had no problem with men per se, so long as they had no romantic ulterior motives. That was the reason why Prince Alexis had chosen us to be his sparring partners—he sensed not one ounce of lust for him in us.

I'd stared off into the distance without realizing it.

Now that I think about it...there used to be more of us common-born new recruits under Prince Alexis's wing.

But the prince found them out sooner or later. One left us, then two... until the only ones left under his command were myself and my colleague.

And where did the dropouts go, you may ask? To the other world, of course. They fell for other men, had their first times, and became gay lovers.

Of course, I was still friends with them. But I felt a distance between us now. If anything, I felt a closer kinship to Prince Alexis.

"This is Prince Alexis we're talking about here, the guy who learned how to swordfight from an early age because sickos kept going after him. To think that the poor guy had to protect his chastity even though he's a guy himself—the royal court really is a terrifying place..." I trailed off and punctuated my thought with a sigh of despair.

When I was his age, I'd wander alone through the woods by my village without a second thought.

"Hey, do you think the story's true? You know, about how Alexis cut off a guy's you-know-what because he was going after him, then he fed it to a dog?"

Just hearing my companion say those words made me squeeze my thighs together.

"I heard that Prince Alexis hasn't been pursued since, so maybe it's true?"

I guess that meant the bastards stopped trying to have their way with him by force. I don't care who you are or who you want—consent is an absolute requirement.

"I wonder if the rumors about Princess Octavia finding out what happened, exploding into a fiery rage, and using her authority to socially assassinate the pedo-bastards are also true... I heard some of them begged her to just kill them instead."

This information from my companion was news to me.

"That would be a befitting end to the pedo-bastards... But would Princess Octavia really—?"

"Just look at that. What a wholesome sight...," my companion interjected.

I followed his gaze and found Princess Octavia and Prince Alexis patting each other's heads. An innocent tender moment between brother and sister, beautiful boy and beautiful girl.

As someone who'd only caught glimpses of her from afar, I had no idea what Princess Octavia's true nature was. The only information I had was rumors I'd heard.

To be sure, when she was younger, she was widely considered a child prodigy, surpassing even the likes of Prince Sirius in intellect. But the older she grew, the dimmer her light became. Almost as if she learned firsthand the dangers of exposing one's true abilities.

Fundamentally, the impression her outward appearance gave did not betray expectations. She was a mild-mannered princess.

However, at times, she would act in very unpredictable ways. Like, for example…choosing the Emissary of Ongarne as her personal bodyguard.

For a start, ever since I got my post at the castle, the princess's bodyguards changed like the wind. Everyone either moved away or transferred amicably. I never heard about any of her former bodyguards being murdered or anything like that.

However… Why did they get replaced so rapidly? Was there perhaps some secret reason that was hidden beneath the surface?

One thing was clear—ever since the Emissary of Ongarne was assigned as her bodyguard, the game of musical chairs had suddenly stopped.

And the Emissary of Ongarne—the man who I still remember clearly stepping over a mound of corpses on the battlefield, smiling eerily, his face stained in blood—was now tamed.

It was almost as if the Emissary of Ongarne was born to be the princess's bodyguard.

And such a one-sided relationship was not sustainable. Wasn't it *only* possible if the princess wished for his service, and the Emissary of Ongarne accepted?

Octavia—Esfia's first princess. She avoided interacting with everyone in her family except Prince Alexis as much as possible, and it was said that she disapproved of Prince Sirius's romance with Lord Sil.

Behind those gentle eyes…she was hungry for the throne. There were whispers of her intentions from a good portion of the castle. And if this were true, that would make the Emissary of Ongarne her first chess move… Her declaration of war.

And when open conflict broke out, there was a 90 percent chance that Prince Alexis would side with Princess Octavia…

It would be Prince Sirius versus Princess Octavia and Prince Alexis. And who would win? From my vantage point…I couldn't be sure.

Maybe Prince Sirius would crush them. There didn't seem to be any way Prince Sirius could lose…but there was a part of me that couldn't fully believe this.

"—!"

A threat suddenly entered my field of vision. There was a sword… flying straight at Princess Octavia.

She wouldn't be mortally wounded, but she still might be hurt. That's what I could judge from the sword's trajectory.

But the sword…was struck down. By the Emissary of Ongarne.

There was an icy gleam in his eye. But his clearly murderous gaze shot straight across the training grounds, piercing the young soldier who'd thrown the sword.

I sized up the sword thrower. Trembling with murderous rage, his face was drained of color, and his legs were wobbling. He was a nobleman— and one of the idiots whose heart burned with savage lust for Prince Alexis.

The lovesick soldier was so far gone that the mere sight of Prince Alexis's sole display of affection for Princess Octavia—his sister— consumed him with malevolence.

So much so that he would let his feelings consume him and commit an impulsive action with complete disregard for the consequences.

Well…he's a goner.

The Emissary of Ongarne wasn't the only person staring daggers in the training grounds. Prince Alexis's malicious gaze joined his. There weren't many things Prince Alexis despised more than getting hurt, but the possibility of his sister getting hurt was definitely one of them. Even if she escaped an attack unscathed.

And in that moment, Prince Alexis held the highest rank in the training grounds. Even though Princess Octavia was older than him, since she was a lady, Prince Alexis's authority took precedence. Prince Alexis would probably sentence him to a beheading then and there.

The training grounds were deathly silent as Prince Alexis picked up the fallen sword.

He spoke, his voice shaking with anger. "Who threw this sword? Step forward and name yourself. Otherwise, I will consider this an attempt on my sister's life."

The malice in the Emissary of Ongarne's eyes vanished. An obvious sign he had yielded the floor to Prince Alexis. He warily guarded Princess Octavia—his movements more pronounced than usual.

I was sure the man who threw the sword wanted to flee...but that would not be permitted. After all, he had attempted to harm a royal. It was clearly intentional, but if he ran away now, he would lose even the chance to try to explain himself, and he would be sentenced to death for the attempted assassination of the princess.

He must have been terribly distraught. The sword thrower fell twice in his attempt to run the very short distance to Prince Alexis. Then he stood before the prince like a condemned man waiting to hear his sentence.

"M-my name is Heller Byrne! Th-that sword b-belongs to me. M-my hand slipped, and I—!"

Before Prince Alexis could answer, Princess Octavia reacted. "Well, now... So it was an accident, then?"

A hushed murmur swept through the training grounds.

Princess Octavia snapped the fan in front of her face closed. "Then it can't be helped. Everyone makes mistakes, Alec. So stop that scowling."

"But...but, Sister, if the worst had happened to you, I...! I cannot overlook this transgression. He must be beheaded!"

"Beheaded... Do you really think that is a fair punishment for this poor soldier's momentary lapse of judgment?"

Of course it wasn't...I suppose.

"I won't forbid you from giving the order. But the punishment should fit the crime, no?"

"D-do you mean it, Princess?" the slimy sword thrower asked her shamelessly.

"Why, yes. I mean what I say. Unless you desire a harsh punishment?" she asked right back.

The sword thrower quickly shook his head. "Oh, thank you, Princess! Words cannot express my grat—"

"That's enough, dear." Princess Octavia smiled brightly. "You hail from House Byrne, yes?"

The sword thrower's grateful eyes clouded over with confusion. "Aye... My father is currently serving Viscount Byrne..."

"And...you have an elder brother, I hear."

The confusion on the attacker's face was suddenly covered with astonishment and caution.

Princess Octavia beckoned the soldier to approach. He hesitated for a moment, but when she motioned for him to hurry, he sidled up to her. It looked like Prince Alexis wanted to stop him, but he could not intervene.

Princess Octavia spread her fan wide...and said something to the sword thrower that only he could hear. And he answered her back. They continued to talk like this for a while, until eventually, they stepped away from each other.

"Well, I do hope you can help me," she told him.

The sword thrower nodded solemnly. "Yes, Your Highness..."

"Sister...," Prince Alexis implored, his brow furrowed.

"He had no intention to harm me. It was an accident—nothing more. But since he insisted on making amends, I asked a little favor of him."

"You asked a favor...from this cad? What kind of—?"

"It's a secret," Princess Octavia interrupted, placing an index finger in front of her lips. "I appreciate your concern. But please...try to not make his punishment too severe, Alec? Consider it a personal favor to me."

Though reluctantly, Prince Alexis nodded in agreement. "Very well... I will instruct the others to do as you say."

And thus, the ruling was made.

"Ah, yes. Alderton?" Lastly, Princess Octavia addressed her bodyguard, the Emissary of Ongarne. "Thank you for protecting me."

"Aye..."

And with that, the princess walked away.

As for the sword thrower—whose name I now knew to be Heller

Byrne—he was sentenced to five hundred practice swings as part of his punishment.

Given what Princess Octavia had said to Prince Alexis, and that Prince Alexis had said he would "instruct the others to do as you say," it made sense why his punishment was so tame.

Consequently, Heller Byrne was not ambushed and beaten half to death in the middle of the night, either. Because anyone who did such a thing would be punished.

After I finished my day's training, I approached the new recruit from my village to ask him some questions.

"Say, is House Byrne well-known?"

Matters of the nobility always bored me to tears. It was fastest to ask an expert.

"Heller, eh? Lucky bastard—talk about a narrow escape. And no, House Byrne isn't all that well-known. Their territory is rather small, you see, and they're far from the royal capital. It's an unremarkable place out in the sticks."

"Know anything about his elder brother?"

"Nah... I don't know that much. But judging by what the princess says, I guess at least he has one."

"Do you think his elder brother is well-known among the nobility?"

"Nah, no clue."

The deeper I dug, the more mysteries I found.

Days later, my colleague and I were assigned to Prince Alexis.

And by the way, neither of us has been influenced by the nobility's philosophy of romance.

And we have no plans of doing so, either.

5

Esfia used the same calendar as modern Japan. There were twenty-four hours in a day, seven days a week, about thirty days per month, and twelve months per year.

Culturally, it was roughly like early modern Europe. We didn't have electricity, but we enjoyed a high level of cuisine, clothing, and housing. The houses in the castle town that I could see from my window were clean. There was an abundance of food. We even had some ingredients that made you go, "*Whoa, are you sure this isn't modern Japan?!*" Like, a dessert would have a different name, but you'd eat it and be like, "*Isn't this the flavor of green tea and rice cakes...just like matcha shiratama ice cream?!*"

Even though this world doesn't have any countries like Japan in it, since it's based off *The Noble King*, a book that was written in Japan, those concepts are pretty malleable.

Which begs the question...why didn't they just invent a potion that could let men get pregnant?! I asked myself this question over and over and *over* again...to no avail.

I mean, this is a fantasy. So why not?

I was back from the training grounds in my cozy room in the castle, just chilling. Let me clarify. I wasn't allowed to just roam around the castle whenever I pleased. I had to stay in my room until six PM. We always had the whole family together for dinner, whenever possible, at seven PM. At nine PM, I had my bath. Bedtime was ten PM, and I woke up at six AM...

A princess's schedule was always set, down to the minute. It was the same for my brothers and parents, though we each had a different schedule.

I sat down in my favorite chair and whispered, "So...I guess I've got a lead on my little problem."

Thanks to the minor mishap in the training grounds, my efforts bore some fruit. That was why my heart was at ease, now that I was back in my room.

And as for that mishap... Well, a sword came flying straight at me, and Alderton swiftly struck it down. I wasn't harmed, but the air in the training ground froze.

Everyone was like... *Was that an attempt on the princess's life?*

Well, the fact of the matter was...a clumsy soldier accidently sent his sword flying in a random direction when he'd tried to draw it. The end!

I mean, when Alec told him to come forward, the guy tripped over his feet twice even though he was only a few meters away. The guy was clearly a klutz.

And even if this all *weren't* the case...whether it was intentional or an accident, I felt like charging him for attempted murder was taking things a bit too far. Though I admit I'm only saying this because I wasn't hurt!

But him turning out to be from House Byrne was a stroke of luck. When I heard his name, a lightbulb flicked on in my head.

I remembered him. Back in *The Noble King*, there was a character called Rust Byrne. He was twenty-six years old.

I needed someone to play my fake boyfriend...and he seemed to be a promising specimen!

Who would play my boyfriend? Or rather, who would be the easiest choice with the least amount of potential drama? And who would be likely to say yes? I went over many scenarios in my brain.

My brothers had many devotees...many allies.

First, there was Team Sil x Sirius. They were always ready to lend a helping hand to those dudes. This was true with most stories, but in *The Noble King*, it was always advantageous to side with the main characters, so they drew in many followers with their influence. And as is always the case with man-on-man couples, some of these devotees were wild stallions with secret feelings for Lord Sil, and others were green-eyed monsters who sought to sow seeds of destruction between Sil and Sirius. And both camps were full of hot ikemen!

Seeing this made me despair more and more... Was there a way for a girl to get her foot in the door? Nope!

So all the gentlemen in Sil and Sirius's camp...were lost causes.

Which meant I had to set my sights on the men who were the villains in the book. Those would be my fake-boyfriend targets. It was the only way.

And since all the noblemen who were antagonistic toward my big brother were...mostly over the age of forty...then I'd go for their sons! Or failing that, their sons' devotees!

So. What kind of people were critical of my big brother?

The answer is actually connected to the question of how the nobility produced blood heirs when man-on-man romances had permeated their culture.

Did the other nobles adopt Esfia's royal family's ways? Not exactly... Well, they did emulate certain aspects of the royal family, but it's not like all their sons married men.

For example, sometimes when the eldest son of a nobleman wanted to marry another man, he was admonished to recall his responsibilities. But it was never like, "*Break up with him at once!*" because...you know, this is a BL world, after all...

So how were they admonished, exactly, you may ask? Can you give me some specifics, you may ask? It would always be this: "*You may have your romance with a man, but you must marry a woman!*"

There was a silent agreement that you couldn't make light of the importance of having a wife. But from the husband's POV, his male lover was his true wife, so in reality, most family dynamics were complicated.

So!

The first time I happened upon an ordinary man-and-woman married couple...their favorability rating skyrocketed in my book. And if I encountered such a couple who happened to still be in love with each other, well, I'd use every bit of my princess privilege to be their biggest cheerleader!

I kinda went overboard with one couple...

But anyway, many noblemen married women for the sole purpose of having kids. Because of this, two major factions occurred among the nobility.

One faction was the True Love Nobles. They believed a nobleman's love for his man conquered all. They'd adopt a child (most commonly from relatives or their sisters, though sometimes they adopted from outside the family from gifted bloodlines, of course), and carry on the family name that way.

The other faction was the Adulterous Nobles. These noblemen married women—in spite of loving men—and kept male lovers outside the home.

I know it sounds like a big joke, but it's real. These two factions are actually a thing. Maybe they keep doing it because they enjoy it? There are other things that divide the nobility into factions, but this matter was the primary thing that split them in two.

Oh, and incidentally, though there's fewer of them percentagewise, the faction with the most influence is the True Love Nobles. After all, polygamy isn't officially legal, and the current king of Esfia—my father—is married to the man he loves.

In my former life, I would've definitely been in the True Love Nobles faction. And in my current life, from Octavia's POV...I'm in the man-parts-ways-with-his-male-lover-after-an-agonizing-deliberation-then-marries-a-woman-then-gradually-finds-and-nurtures-a-true-love-with-his-wife faction!

And would you believe it—such a happy-medium noble family does indeed exist! They're House Nightfellow. Unfortunately, Duke Nightfellow's son seems to be in the True Love faction...but he's a friend of Sirius, you see. I guess the duke didn't pass on his ideology to his son.

Sooo... To sum up, the Esfian nobles' propensity for romance is divided between the True Love Nobles, the Adulterous Nobles, and Other. (Like the Nightfellows or men who actually married women for love.)

In *The Noble King*, the True Love Nobles were the main focus, and they were all on Team Sil x Sirius. You couldn't say that all the Adulterous Nobles were their enemies, but they weren't exactly painted in a good light in the novel, and that trend seemed to be consistent with real life in Esfia. From a woman's point of view, it was like there would inevitably be a moment of: *"Don't tell me he's your lover?!"* It was very frustrating.

But as a princess, I have something I wish to say... Those men have their merits!

Like, that they're critical of same-sex marriage among royalty! I mean, can you blame them, when they were forced to marry women they didn't love out of a sense of duty? Even though they may turn a blind eye to my brother and Sil, they do often complain that noblemen should just suck it up and do it with a woman. It would certainly help solve the whole heir issue in the future!

Ergo, I needed someone who didn't have his foot in my brother's camp and who was also in the Adulterous Noble Faction. It was the only logical answer.

Now, truth be told, I'd rather go with someone in the Other camp, like a Nightfellow. But even though it was clear a man was in that camp if he was happily married to a woman whom he loved with all his heart...if a man was unmarried, it was a mystery which faction he was in. Noblemen who only preferred women weren't exactly public with that information until they were married to one. So they were impossible to distinguish from the Adulterous Noble Faction!

In conclusion, I needed to get someone around my age from the Adulterous Noble Faction to agree to pretend to be my boyfriend! Yup, let's go with that!

It sounded good in my head when I got that far in my thoughts... but I quickly hit a wall: Most Adulterous Noble faction men my age were already taken!

Well, of course they were... They're the sort of people who deliberately make a choice to marry women.

Not to mention, even if such a guy did exist, it's not like I'd be able to casually meet up with him for a friendly chat. And as for a guy I could meet up with in secret and be like, "*You're my pretend-boyfriend! 'K, thanks, bye!*" ...Yeah, no such guy exists.

But the klutzy soldier dropped a potential lead right into my lap! Rust Byrne. He was in the Adulterous Noble Faction, but he was still only twenty-six years old and a bachelor. He and my big brother had had a slightly hostile relationship in the past, which sent him into hiding. He was a sub-character who only came out during key points in the story.

Duke Byrne treated Rust like a tumor. But according to *The Noble King*, his little brother Heller was in regular contact with Rust.

And so, back at the training grounds, I gave Heller the chance of a lifetime by asking him to connect me with his brother. However, when Alec asked me directly what I'd requested of Heller, I panicked.

There's no way I can tell him.

Unable to come up with a good excuse, I eventually went with a vague "It's a secret" answer. Which, now that I think about it, probably just made the whole thing seem more curious to him...

I have a feeling I chose my answer unwisely. I hope everything'll work out okay...

Anyway, Heller did agree to my request, so I should receive a letter from Rust Byrne pretty soon. I intend to meet with him face-to-face and go into negotiations from there.

But...

I tensed up.

I know I'm in uncharted waters here, but I shouldn't rest on my laurels just because I thought I found a ray of hope in Rust. Whether my negotiations with Rust go well or not...well, that's another matter entirely.

Which means, it's time to work on Plan B!

I need to be proactive—roam around and find some more potential fake boyfriends... This means going to social gatherings where Adulterous Nobles would be, or to those nobility-sponsored junior balls I'm always invited to but turn down... I'm about to be constantly on the move!

"Wait... 'Move'?"

Huh?

I sat up with a start, realizing I'd forgotten something very important.

If I got a new bodyguard…wouldn't that completely trap me?

The transition period between the predecessor's resignation and the official appointment of my new bodyguard was at least a week. Usually two weeks. At most, three months.

First, there was the selection process…then, even when one was finalized, it sometimes took a few days before he officially started working for me.

The changing of the guard took time. And during that time, I was forbidden to go outside the castle walls. Even my mobility within the castle was limited.

Additionally, during the transitional period when I had no official bodyguard, substitute guards would be assigned to me concurrently. Part-time bodyguards, so to speak. There would be a great many of them sharing the duty of guarding me.

However, from a safety standpoint, I was encouraged to limit my own movements until my new bodyguard was officially appointed.

And my official bodyguard…would always disappear suddenly.

It was just a way of life for me up until now. But now…a changing of the guard would throw a major wrench in my plans. After experiencing confinement time after time after time…I know all too well.

If Alderton (whose name I had only learned today) were to quit now… I'd be plunged into transition limbo, and seeking a fake romance would be absolutely impossible.

I pictured Alderton's face in my mind. Anyone would agree he's a fine specimen!

Urrrgh. No matter how you look at it, it's a miracle he hasn't already hooked up with somebody! Like, he might run off tomorrow, for all I know. I can see it now: Alderton, with his boyfriend on his arm, giving me his letter of resignation… It's scary just how clearly I can picture the scene!

I shook my head vehemently. Then I thought back to how he'd served me all this time as my bodyguard. From my vantage point, I didn't see any indication that he would quit, from the way he served me. And I never got the sense that Alderton was falling for his one true love... The changing of the guard was, after all, always initiated by the guard falling in love with someone.

So maybe...I should casually ask him about it? No, no, it's time to throw your shame out the window, Octavia! Just ask him, "Do you plan on resigning?" *plain and simple.*

And if he does plan on resigning, I'll just make him agree to stick it out with me for another month, no matter what. Yeah, that's what I'll do.

Well, let's strike while the iron's hot.

And with that, I rang my call bell.

6

In a flash, my handmaid popped into my room. "You rang, Your Highness?"

Sasha had been my handmaid for half a year now. Her blond hair was in an updo, and her voluptuous body was clothed in her castle-issued maid uniform. She was twenty-six years old, and an alluring fragrance wafted from her deceptively conservative and tidy figure. I'd definitely describe her as sexy rather than pretty. If I were a man, I would've definitely been seducing her right now.

"I have an urgent request for—" I cut off when I saw Sasha's face.

I almost shrieked, "*Nooo!*" out loud.

Sasha's eyes were abnormally white—like a dead fish! No...more like a dead fish that's already started to rot!

There was only one reason for Sasha—or any of the other initiated castle handmaids—to get such a look in their eyes.

"Oh, Sasha...I'm so sorry, dear. Did my sudden summons cause you to see something objectionable?"

"Of course not, my lady! It was not your fault, Your Highness... It's just, the probability of a chance encounter with him was high today," Sasha explained, slapping her cheeks. She was trying to ease the tension in her face.

"Ah, so that's all it was..."

"Yes, my lady..."

When handmaids begin their service at the castle, their eyes generally sparkle at first. Since the post is attained through a test, handmaids come from a variety of backgrounds. The pay is good, and there's ample opportunity for a handmaid to network. For a woman, the castle is the ideal place for her to work.

And naturally, their hearts flutter with hopes of romance on the horizon! Even the common soldiers are generally blessed with handsomeness here. So the handmaids invariably fall in love. It may sound rash, but any girl would get her hopes up when surrounded by all those hot gentlemen...

He's always so nice to me... Do I have a chance with him? would lead to frequent chats, stalking him during his breaks, sometimes giving him little snacks... Every handmaid—the uninitiated ones, that is—always fangirls so hard.

Handmaids who have undergone The Initiation never say anything... either out of kindness or due to whatever their personal experience was. Nobody would believe their tragic tales anyway. People believe what they want to believe. Besides, if a girl is having a happy dream, she's better off staying asleep...because the day will come when she'll be rudely awakened.

Sometimes it'd be her crush in a love scene, sometimes a bedroom scene, sometimes a lovers' quarrel...and she'd walk in on it by chance.

All of these scenarios would be man-on-man, of course.

Just like me, these poor handmaids would be thwarted in love...and not by other women, but by men!

In time, the majority of the handmaids (especially the ones who came here looking for a love connection) would gradually lose the light in their eyes. It goes without saying that if you want any chance of finding a husband, you're better off forgetting the castle and just sticking with your home village.

Whenever a handmaid witnessed a secret tryst between two men, the darkness in her eyes would grow even darker. And when they got back to work with their dead-fish eyes, they'd become hardworking supermaids. My current chief lady-in-waiting, Matilda, was that very type.

Poor Sasha had cried her eyes out on her Day of Discovery.

"Your Highness...I await your command," Sasha said. *Please don't make me talk about it,* her stiff gaze finished.

"I want you to go to my chief lady-in-waiting and gather as many documents as you can from the background check of my bodyguard...of Alderton...as quickly as possible."

"Right away, my lady," Sasha said, bowing and leaving the room.

She returned promptly and handed me the documents I'd requested. *Okay...let's do a little light reading.*

Klifford Alderton. Twenty-five years old. About a year ago, at the request of Count Alderton—both he and his house were renowned for militaristic prowess—he was adopted into House Alderton. He was originally a commoner from Turchen. He became a candidate for my bodyguard on recommendation from Count Alderton and also on merit. Interestingly enough, he scored lowest in the practical exam in the final round of the selection process.

After reading through all the documents about Alderton, it started to make sense.

Aha...so that's his story.

Maybe that's why Alec had called Alderton "you bastard." Maybe it's because he knew the guy's history.

The real curveball is that he's from Turchen.

Turchen was a territory along the border of the neighboring kingdom of Khangena, and up until about a century ago, it belonged to Khangena...until Esfia annexed it after committing some pretty nasty atrocities, from what I've heard.

Because of this, anti-Esfian sentiment was rampant among the Turchen people. I learned about this in my royal lessons. My teacher had told me in a hushed whisper, *"It's best you call them not Esfians but Turchens."*

Turchen, huh...?

When I was reading *The Noble King*, the story had just gotten to the Turchen Arc...but while I was eagerly waiting for the release of the next volume, I just had to go and die.

Man, I remember there was an incident in the Turchen Arc where the keyword *Ongarne* came up. I was crazy excited to find out what happened next... Oh, right! When I became Octavia, the meaning behind the word Ongarne did become somewhat clearer to me. It's this religion's version of...Hell? That's their name for it.

After some pondering, I reached my conclusion: *So what?*

I mean, I didn't know what Ongarne was when I read the books, and it's still a mystery to me now. I think there must be something more to it. I mean, if it's just their name for Hell, you can't go there without dying, can you?!

Wait, I did die, though...

A sigh fell out of my mouth... I was so confused.

Hmm... I'm really in a pickle, aren't I?

I'd hoped to gather a bit of information on Alderton before I interviewed him. But if anything, I felt like I got some bad information...

Especially him being from Turchen... And him scoring last place in the practical exam.

I could never really picture him coming last in anything. And with Count Alderton's seal of approval, he's sure to be gifted. If the Count's acclamations of his adoptive son turned out to be untrue, well, that would certainly tarnish his and his house's social standing.

All of my bodyguard candidates were skilled—that was a given. Even so, Alderton? Last place?

It's hard to believe this is the guy who's been guarding me the past three months. It would've been much more natural for him to have taken the top spot in the rankings.

Which begged the question...

"Did he score last place...on purpose?"

That seemed the most plausible. In other words, Alderton's heart wasn't in the game! He didn't want to be chosen as my bodyguard, so he slacked off.

And yet he was still chosen.

So...is that the gist of it?

There was a knock at my door then.

"This is Klifford Alderton. I was informed by your handmaid that you required my presence."

Here we go!

I'm kinda nervous. Since I uncovered this shocking truth, I feel like I'm going up against the final boss...

I swallowed hard, filed away the documents in my desk, and grabbed my fan. My fan—it was like a part of me. I could shut out prying eyes and hide my own emotions—holding it always put me at ease.

"Why, yes, come in. You have permission to enter my chambers."

Alderton entered my bedchamber. So as not to be rude to me, he quickly scanned the room, furrowing his brow a little. That move was top-tier swoon-worthy—I wouldn't be surprised if he hooked up with someone (a guy) as early as tomorrow.

Alderton stayed close to my door and said, "Your Highness, forgive my asking, but are you certain you do not wish the presence of your handmaid? You wish to be alone with me?"

Well...yeah?

I just stared at him at first. I honestly didn't know what he was trying to say.

My handmaid? Does he mean Sasha? "You wish to be alone with me?" ...Heh?

Ohhh! Now I get it!

I smirked, "There is nothing wrong, Alderton." I nodded firmly for good measure.

Even though I had strong suspicions that Alderton hadn't wanted to become my bodyguard, he was still quite good at it. My calling him into my bedchamber alone probably struck him as suspicious.

I grabbed the teapot that Sasha had brought in to pour some tea. Two ceramic cups sat on the table beside it. I discarded my fan long enough to perform this basic act of hospitality before picking it up again. Alderton watched in silence.

"What do you mean by...there is nothing wrong?" he asked.

"It means that I trust you."

An unmarried woman and man—princess and personal bodyguard aside—were alone in her bedchamber when there wasn't an emergency. That sort of thing basically never happened.

When a princess was in her personal quarters, her handmaid would always keep an eye on her so that nothing disgraceful could occur.

But you see...Esfia's history tells a different story. For a princess, the one who can give her true assurances and safety is her bodyguard! For example, I doubt it'd be a problem if they even spent a night in the same bed together! Has there ever been a bodyguard who got into some risky business with his princess...? Nope! Not a one!

At least, I haven't found a single instance of it in my research. When I fell in love with my bodyguard in the past, I wondered, *Hasn't a princess ever hooked up with her bodyguard before?* I had scoured the books in the castle library for days on end until my eyes were bloodshot trying to find the answer!

But what I did find were some brutally honest diaries written by former court ladies, probably as a warning to their successors. And ohhh boy, did they spill some tea. There was many a tale of unrequited love from my ancestors. One of my ancestors even latched on to her bodyguard stark naked. What happened next, you ask? She was coldly rejected, apparently. The page the story was written on had tearstains on it... Oh, my poor ancestors!

Bodyguards were impregnable fortresses. When it came to their princesses, they had willpowers of steel. Princesses were safe around them.

But as for princes... Well, my big brother was probably in the clear because he was attached to Lord Sil, but Alec was in danger. If a prince and his bodyguard ever found themselves alone behind a closed door... there was a good chance something would happen. The diary I read even said so. Seriously, Alec was in much more danger than I was. Like, ten times as much danger...maybe even more.

"You trust me...?"

Hmm? Alderton's eyes were emotionless, but there was a hint of cynicism in his voice.

"Yes, I do."

"You do say some truly amusing things sometimes, Your Highness," he said, his lips twisting slightly upward.

There it was. That smile I thought I saw when we were on the training grounds.

"Do I?"

I was being totally serious, though!

Then he said nothing.

And I said nothing...

G-God, this silence is painful!

This was a job for...The Fan. I flicked it open with a flourish. I'm actually pretty picky when it comes to fan opening. You've gotta do it with style!

I first started using my fan because Octavia used one in *The Noble King*, so I figured I might as well, too. On the cover art of the light novels, she used a high-quality fan made of bright white feathers. But it was *hella* hard to use. It was also heavy, and it kinda really reeked!

So the fan I use now is custom-made from a bird that sheds large quantities of feathers when it's molting. It comes from the kind of large bird you'd see flying around anywhere, but the feathers are very special. You see, they are jet-black, lightweight, and fluffy. They are heaven to touch. So I was confused when I asked a craftsman to make me a fan out of these feathers and he made a face and said, *"But they're black... Are you sure you want me to use feathers from this bird? Forgive me for being crass, but are you serious?"* It was a very painful memory, but I won't let it get to me!

I can open and close it in a flash! And yet…when it's open, it's so soft. Sometimes, I just nuzzle my cheek up against it.

Now that my fan was open and I was relaxed, I gestured toward the seat across from me. "Have a seat, Alderton," I said.

I even had some tea on standby. I may have prepared it myself, but it wasn't that bad…I hoped. Even coddled princesses had a certain degree of domestic competency. We had to throw tea parties, after all.

"Aye…," Alderton said, finally pulling himself away from the door. But he wouldn't sit in the chair I'd offered; instead, he stood directly behind it.

"I hope this is satisfactory, Your Highness," he said with a formal bow.

Operation Lighten Up the Mood with Kindness…was an epic fail!

I guess I'll just have to use the direct approach after all… Geez, I'm nervous…

I switched my fan over to my left hand. I felt his hard gaze on me as I lifted my teacup to my mouth with my right…

And as I felt the tea loosen up my vocal cords, I brought my fan to my cheek and looked up at Alderton. "So…do you plan on resigning soon?"

So…do you have a crush on somebody?

7

"And…what makes you ask that?" Alderton asked right back without batting an eye.

Yep…so polite. He's always so polite. But, and this might just be my paranoia talking, I'm sensing major "What the hell's wrong with this chick?" vibes from Alderton. If he's giving off those vibes because he doesn't want to quit, then I'm a happy girl, but I don't get that sense from him…

However! I mustn't falter! Behold my mighty princess spirit!

I covered my face with my fan. *God, these fluffy feathers rock.* "I meant every word. I had a sudden worry that you might resign. Tell me the truth…you never wanted to be my bodyguard, right?"

Alderton shook his head. "What a preposterous notion."

Well, I guess it's normal to deny an accusation like that.

"Then can you explain your performance in the practical exam?"

The room fell silent. Did his lack of a prompt answer mean my theory was correct? Alderton continued to stare at me in silence—a silence that was oddly intimidating…

"Um… I need you to answer me, or I'll never understand why."

And finally, Alderton spoke. "No…I need *your* answer, Your Highness," he began, his blue eyes piercing me as he stared right into mine. "Why did you choose me?"

I almost piped up with, "*Why, with my special technique: eeny-meeny-miny-moe!*" But I bit my tongue.

Instead, I answered, "It was an oracle from the Sky."

Yup. I made the right move.

For a moment, all traces of emotion left Alderton's face.

What's this…? Did I say something taboo? But "It was an oracle from the Sky" is a common saying in Esfia, y'know? It's like our catchphrase!

Esfia had many religions, but even though each had their own name for it, they all actually worshipped the same god. Like, a sky god? We use the word *Sky* to refer to God—it even comes up in casual conversation! Even Turchens know about it, my dude.

"Of all the things you could say…it was an oracle from the Sky?"

While I was having an internal panic attack, Alderton's chest heaved in a deep chuckle. And a macho smirk spread on his sinfully handsome face.

Aha. Now I finally see that Alderton is a commoner.

Up until then, from the way he moved and acted, he looked like he became a nobleman and a knight before he could even crawl.

But now he looks…savage? Like a wild beast. That's not the kind of vibe a trueborn nobleman could give off so easily.

"I see. So you have no answer for me, Your Highness," he answered, reverting to model knight.

"Oh, I will tell you why I asked if you intended to resign. Alderton... are you aware that I tend to go through bodyguards quickly?"

"Yes, I am aware of that," he answered dutifully. This gave me pause.

"Well, watching you work the past three months gave me an idea. This changing of the guard that has been such a big part of my life...I want it to end with you."

It's a done deal, okay? I finished with my eyes.

Alderton's eyes widened slightly.

In my past life, I had seen this play out in a manga. Whenever you negotiate, always highball your opponent! If you want to sell something for five hundred yen, always start the bidding with one thousand! Then you can play the victim as you lower the price. And in the end, you make a sale for six hundred yen! Now, that's business, baby!

In my case, I wanted Alderton to continue being my bodyguard for at least one more month, but since I determined that Alderton secretly hated his job, I set the bar all the way up at *"Serve me for the rest of your life!"*

Then Alderton would be like, *"The rest of my life? You've gotta be kidding me!"*

Then I'd whisper sweetly, *"Okay, then how about one month? But you'd better promise not to quit on me if you get a boyfriend during that time,"* as a compromise.

Then Alderton was sure to go, *"Oh, just one month? That's easy!"*

Now, your move, my opponent!

My opponent...Alderton...got an amused look on his face for some reason. I could tell from the angle of his lips.

He looks amused... Huh? Wait, isn't that weird? But I can at least consider his reaction positive, right? It wasn't the reaction I was anticipating, but if it's positive, then I'm totally cool with it.

"You want me to be your last... Does this mean you're asking me to serve you indefinitely?"

"Why, yes."

If you're fine with serving me for all time, I'm a happy girl. Bring it!

"It pains me to say this, Your Highness...but it seems as though you do not realize the weight those words carry."

"Oh...don't I?"

Well, that's outrageous. I totally do know!

"Wouldn't that mean you serving me for the rest of your life? As long as it means you won't resign, I'm fine with it," I answered.

Alderton bowed his head. "If that is what you wish...then your wish is my command."

I snapped my fan closed. "So you'll keep serving me, yes?"

"As long as you wish me to, Your Highness."

All riiiight! He can't back out now!

In my past life, I would've made him sign something at this point. When I was Maki Tazawa, my father, mother, big sister, and I rented a condo. And when it came time to renew our lease, we always got a new contract to sign. Yes, that. A contract! That's what I'm talking about. But there aren't exactly contracts between bodyguard and princess.

What can we use as a contract...?

I remembered how Alderton refused to tell Alec his name due to Esfia's old custom. This guy did seem to be a stickler for tradition.

"I am pleased. Now, shall we conduct the oath ritual?" I suggested, setting down my fan and rising to my feet.

I know *oath ritual* sounded official and cool and all, but it's actually gonna be a present! Whenever a lord and a vassal shared a promise, the lord would give the vassal one of his personal items to keep. It's like, "*See? I gave you a present, so keep your promise!*" I guess...it's technically a bribe?

Okay, just kidding. Most vassals in the past were actually impoverished, so lords would put on airs by having their vassals display jewels or other fancy accessories on their feet. And I guess the vassals kinda didn't mind the gesture? I mean, wouldn't you be inspired to serve your lord forever? I know I would. I love getting stuff.

Hmm... But I don't exactly know what sort of stuff Alderton wants.

"Alderton, is there something you desire?" I asked cheerfully.

"Would you...allow me to touch your hand, Your Highness?"

"Why, yes. Of course."

I faced Alderton and offered my right hand, innocently thinking to myself, *Ooh, does he wanna shake hands?* Then I froze.

Alderton dropped to one knee.

Uh…what?

From his knelt position, Alderton gracefully took my hand in his.

"What're you…?"

Wait, is he…?

"I offer you…my Insignia."

And with that, his lips fell onto my right hand. A spark of pain surged through me…along with a heat much warmer than a human body should make.

I gasped.

Alderton…what did you just say?

"*I offer you my Insignia.*"

Insignia…? By Insignia, he couldn't mean…

A complex shape was glowing on my hand. It flashed for an instant, then vanished. It was a pattern that I had seen before, in a book in my royal lessons.

His lips had parted from my hand, but Alderton was still kneeling… and he was still holding my hand.

"Alderton…are you an Adjutant?"

He answered promptly. "Yes. I thought you already knew that, Your Highness."

"No…" I found one *no* wasn't nearly enough, so I added, "No. I had no idea."

"Is that so? But when you commanded that I serve you for life, I just assumed you did so knowing that I was an Adjutant. Was that unnecessary, Your Highness?"

"Unnecessary" doesn't even begin to describe it, pal!

"This is not my problem but yours. This symbol…this Insignia, isn't it incredibly significant to you Adjutants?"

"Rest at ease. Even among Adjutants, I am unique."

"Unique…how?"

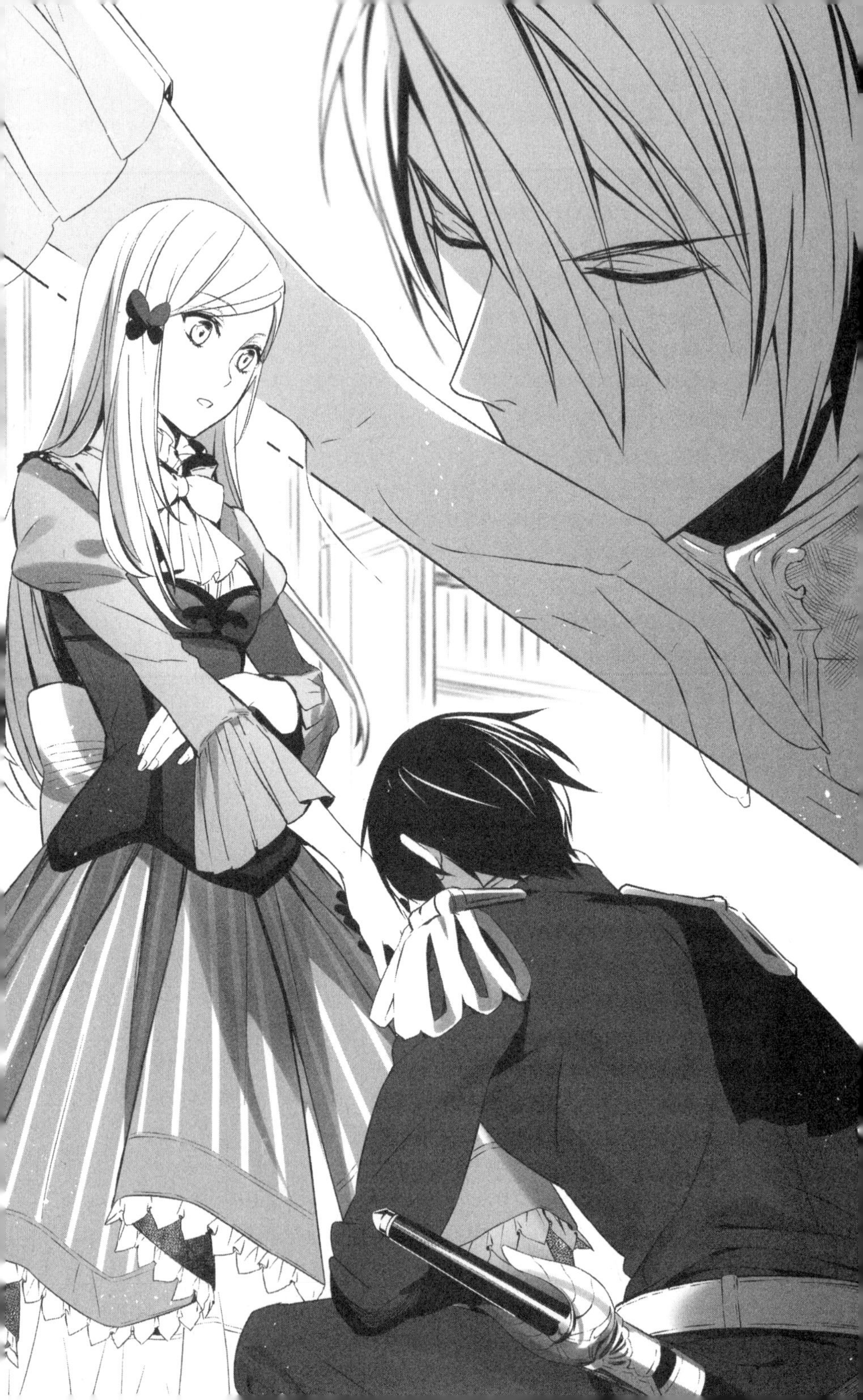

"Well, you are my second Sovereign, Your Highness."

"Is that...even possible?"

An Adjutant was a member of a warrior tribe whose life's mission was to serve his one Sovereign. A Sovereign needn't be an actual king or even royalty. Anyone an Adjutant deemed worthy of being his Sovereign qualified. They could be farmers or merchants—so long as they were compatible with the Adjutant. That was essential.

If both parties consented to the arrangement, an Adjutant would mark his Sovereign with his Insignia. This created an unshakable, special bond between the two. The light from Alderton's Insignia was gone—I couldn't see it, and neither could anyone else. But an Adjutant can see the Insignia. And an Adjutant can use the Insignia to tell him whenever his Sovereign is in danger. This way, an Adjutant could aid his Sovereign, both openly and secretly.

In *The Noble King*—or in Esfia, at least—there was no such thing as magic. But there was one entity that possessed mysterious powers...an Adjutant. And there were still many things unknown about them.

It was also written that an Adjutant could become stronger or weaker, depending on who his Sovereign was. And Turchen was the place that was home to the most Adjutants. They were highly decorated during the war. But at present, there were hardly any of them left.

I'm not sure what percent of the population was made up of Adjutants, but they're basically an endangered species. There was a time when having an Adjutant serve you was a real status symbol among the powerful. But Adjutants only choose their Sovereigns by their own free will. Makes you wonder what happens to Adjutants who fall out of their Sovereign's favor...

Incidentally, according to my royal lessons, there was a rule that an Adjutant could only have one Sovereign for life.

To think that a real-life Adjutant was in my midst all this time...that I already knew him. And what's more, that I'm now his Sovereign. I couldn't help but stare hard at my hand, even though the Insignia was long gone.

Wait a minute... Did I even consent to the Insignia?

"All right, now I understand that you are an eccentric Adjutant. However, did I actually consent to receiving your Insignia?"

I realized I was glaring at Alderton. It kinda irked me that he sprung all this on me. He claimed he thought I knew he was an Adjutant...but maybe he was lying?

"But, Your Highness, you said you wished to give me what I desired. And I desired to give you my Insignia and make you my Sovereign."

"Was that wrong of me?" is what Alderton was shamelessly saying.

Yes, it was wrong!

If you'd clarified what was happening before the deed, I definitely would've pumped the brakes! Well...yeah, I might've said yes anyway, but a girl needs to mentally prepare herself, you know?

However.

"I see..." I sighed, losing the urge to yell at him.

I mean, really, this arrangement has no negatives for me... If anything, since we're now connected by Alderton's Insignia, if I'm ever in danger, he'll know right away and come rescue me. And an Adjutant never abandons his Sovereign. That means as long as I wish it of him, he'll effectively have no choice but to keep his promise of staying my bodyguard.

If anything, won't Alderton lose out on this arrangement? The only positive attribute I can confidently say I have is that I'm a princess! All I have is status! Oh...and I'm also easy on the eyes, I guess!

If I'm an awkward Sovereign...won't that negatively influence my Adjutant? Didn't you jump the gun there, Alderton? Don't come crying to me later about this!

"Does anyone else know that you are an Adjutant?" I asked.

Alderton looked up at me. "Does that include the dead?"

Not cool, Alderton! Way to creep me out!

"Please include only the living in your answer."

"Then it is only you, Your Highness."

"My father...the king, does he know?"

Hmm... Is this maybe all getting a bit too complicated?

"He doesn't. After all, there's no way to detect Adjutants from looks alone. Nobody can tell what I am unless I choose to reveal it."

By suddenly branding them with your Insignia, I suppose!

"Did you not worry that I, your Sovereign, might broadcast the news to everyone?"

Alderton smirked—that slightly twisted smirk of his.

"As you wish, Your Highness."

"Well…I have no intention of telling anyone."

Well, duh! If I've got a secret, I'm the type who will take it to the grave.

"Alderton, I command you not to reveal to anyone else who you are."

"Aye."

I wouldn't mind Alec finding out…but Alec didn't seem to trust Alderton, and if he found out about the whole Adjutant thing, he'd probably just worry even more about me…

"Your Highness," Alderton called to me. This time, he planted a kiss on my right hand.

"!"

Whoa there! Isn't this just like a princess and a handsome knight in a fairy tale—wait, yeah, it's exactly that, but still!

As I stood there, probably blushing a little, Alderton removed his lips from my hand and said, "As an Adjutant, I will protect you with my life, Sovereign. However…I have one warning for you."

Warning?

"I am a unique Adjutant. Do not take my service lightly. Please make use of me as you wish."

"All right… Understood, Al—"

I almost finished my sentence with "Alderton." But then I realized I had no need to distance him by using his surname anymore. The only reason I never bothered to learn my bodyguards' names in the first place was because they'd always quit on me.

His name was Klifford… It was a name I'd only just learned earlier that day, but ever since I read it in his documents, I never forgot it.

"Klifford… Yes, as a sign of trust, I will call you Klifford from now on."

It was time to remember not only his surname but his first name as well. And trust that he was going to be with me for a very long time!

"I am honored…my Sovereign."

And then Alderton...Klifford...gave me the friendliest smile I'd ever seen on him.

8

After the ceremony marking the start of Klifford's...lifetime employment?... Anyway, once that was over, it was about time for dinner, so I proceeded to the castle banquet hall.

It was ornately furnished but cozy, with an oblong dining table draped in a lace tablecloth. There was a chair for every member of the family, and our places at the table were fixed. Father sat at the head of the table. To his right was myself, followed by Alec. On his left, my adoptive (male) mother, then Sirius.

In the not-so-distant future, Lord Sil would also join us. My and Alec's places wouldn't change, but the head of the table would hold our parents, then Sirius on their direct left, followed by Sil.

We all ate the same meal, which was more or less three courses. We'd have soup or salad, a main course, and finish with dessert—all in that order. We used a knife, fork, and spoon to eat.

Our meals were made with the best seasonal produce and fresh meat and fish, and the desserts were always both a feast for the eyes and the stomach. Also, there was always bread. And it was always that round, hard kind of roll that I didn't care for much in my past life. It's even harder than French bread. But it's fragrant, and I love it. Sometimes, I even have seconds!

With the castle chefs putting their craft on full display, it's no wonder that I ate very well every day.

But sometimes...I kinda wished they'd bring out a big variety of dishes and I could choose what I wanted to eat from the bunch. I also kinda wished the menu could be a bit...cheaper? You know, like a cheap restaurant?

Yeah, I know, I need to check my privilege. But after living as a princess for sixteen years, I learned something: Humans can get bored of luxury! It kinda makes you want to do the opposite and eat some light and cheap street food (in Japanese prices, I'm talking about three hundred and fifty yen—in Esfia's currency, that'd be about ten sels.) As much as I love high-end steak...I also love me some takoyaki. When you're surrounded by grade A gourmet...you start to crave grade B. Humans are bottomless pits of greed, aren't we?

When I entered the banquet hall, the others were already there. My family was seated at the table, and their servants and guards lined the wall behind them. Klifford was on standby with the other bodyguards.

This was how Esfian royalty ate—stared at firmly by a bunch of people. So I ate just as elegantly and beautifully as the rest of them. But sometimes, I kinda wished I could chew with my mouth open...

I handed my fan over to the waiter for safekeeping. A servant pulled out my chair for me to sit. I looked over at Alec beside me, and we exchanged smiles.

I turned to face the front where Sirius sat...but we both acted as though our little exchange earlier today hadn't happened. I know I said my plan was to avoid my big brother until I could introduce him to my (fake) boyfriend...but actually, we saw each other every day like this for dinner anyway.

But only certain topics of conversation were considered proper mealtime fare, and knowing my family's dynamic, I highly doubted that Sirius would lay out all our drama. So as long as I could avoid Sirius stopping me after dinner, I'd be scot-free!

"Now that everyone is here..."

My father gave thanks to the Sky God, signaling the commencement of dinner...and the commencement of family conversation. In Esfia, dinner is supposed to be a joyous time where people should talk to each other. But in our family, one misstep from any of us, and we'd wind up eating in silence.

My father and big brother were both the strong, silent type. And while Alec and I were quite chummy outside of formal gatherings, neither of us was much of a conversation starter at dinner. And there was a reason behind this.

There's something about me—I've been this way since I was Maki Tazawa—but I just want to devote myself entirely to my meal when I'm eating! Conversation? Such trivialities are meaningless to me! I simply wish to give the food and my taste buds my full attention!

And as for Alec...well, he tends to walk on eggshells around Father. And I've told him countless times that he shouldn't worry about that, but it's no good for him to hear that from me—he needs his father's permission to speak for it to count...

So that's why most of us never started casually chatting at our dinner table. You'd just strike out. There was really only one person left who could start a conversation... Usually, the first voice to speak up would be my adoptive mother and Father's partner.

His name was Edgar, and I called him Lord Edgar. He was a former merchant, and he had a very attractive personality. Everyone—including the king—was drawn to his imposing talents. He looked young for his age, with wild dark-brown locks and matching eyes. Glasses were his trademark.

The day's dinner conversation, as usual, started with Edgar. "Oh, yes, Sirius. I heard that you and Sil quarreled earlier today?"

I was already sipping the sparkling water the waiter had brought me. In Esfia, sparkling water was a more common accompaniment to a meal than plain water. I really liked the fruit-flavored varieties. Lemon was my go-to!

"So you heard..." Sirius snorted.

Well, of course he heard; a hallway is a pretty exposing place to have PDA, my dude. And you know...even though I'd never do something like that myself, a part of me kinda envied them. To love each other so deeply that you don't care who's watching... I wanted to have a romance like that, too!

"We patched things up, but Octavia gave us a scolding," Sirius said.

All eyes at the table turned on me.

Okay, time to double down! "Well, I had to speak up. Nobody else would."

"You're right," Sirius said. "I was careless. Also, I wanted to say..."

What's this? Sirius is tripping over his words? Don't see that every day.

"Octavia...please forgive me," he apologized, interrupting my pondering.

"Dear Brother...whatever for?"

"For what happened after you scolded me," Sirius answered, looking oddly solemn.

"After...?" I murmured.

Does he mean the part where I got really pissed off? Huh? Wait a minute... I think I know how this is playing out. I've got a bad feeling about this. Can ya maybe not, Sirius?

"I had no idea you had a beloved. It was only natural for my insensitive remark to anger you so. Sil rebuked me for that as well. You...must have been hiding it for so long."

Pfft!

I almost spat out my sparkling water. But I saved face as a princess should and managed (barely) to swallow it back down.

Alec sharply turned to me. "Dear Sister...you have a lover?"

All I could do was stare at Sirius, my jaw on the floor. *Um, excuse me, what kind of plot twist is this?!*

"I want to do what I can to help you, Octavia," Sirius continued. "You kept this from Father, too, right? I wanted to intervene on your behalf as soon as possible...so I decided to announce it here, at dinner."

Dear Brother! Lord Sil affects you too strongly! That's one hell of an over-apology! Did you really have to announce it at the family dinner table?!

No mistaking it, he has good intentions. But here's the catch: I'm not actually in a mutually loving relationship with a man!

"I was worried," Sirius explained, "that perhaps you were keeping your own romance a secret on account of me and Sil?"

"......"

So it's true that people forget how to talk when they're shocked.

"Sirius, Octavia, what is going on here?" our father asked authoritatively.

My father—King Enoch—had an expression very similar to Alec's. His abilities as king were highly lauded. And if I had to give a list of his many shortcomings...most of them would have something to do with Alec.

As I sat there, trying to come up with an excuse, Sirius answered without hesitation. "Octavia has a lover, Father. For a certain reason, I learned of him today. But she wouldn't—that is, she couldn't make the news public because of me. Or perhaps there are some other obstacles, such as his social standing, but, Father... Your Majesty, won't you give Octavia's lover your blessing as king? I wish to give him mine."

Yaaarrrggghhh! Sirius just got serious! He's calling our dad Your Majesty nooow! Which means he's asking for a blessing not as a son to a father but as crown prince to the kiiing!

"Oh, uh, dear Brother!" I stammered, trying to stop him.

But my brother always acted swiftly. And once he made up his mind, he wasn't the type of man who would hesitate to act. He would hesitate to hesitate!

"If Octavia has a beloved, then she has a right to be with him," Sirius implored.

But our father was not so sympathetic. "But we do not even know who he is..."

Sirius stood his ground. "Then why not arrange for a formal introduction? Just among the family, of course."

Wh-whoa now... The situation was spiraling out of my control at lightning speed. *My stomach... It hurts so bad.*

My smug, face-saving lie had taken on a life of its own!

All I wanted to do was show my (fake) boyfriend just to Sirius so I could rub it in his face and be like, *"See?! I'm in a relationship, too! I do love someone, so ha!"*

But if we have a meet-the-parents scenario...there's nowhere to run! I've gotta stop this!

"Th-there is no need for that, dear Brother."

"But why? Octavia...," Sirius asked, shaking his head in disbelief.

"Because I do not wish to inconvenience my beloved..." *Who doesn't even slightly exist yet!* I finished in my head. If I had to name a name at this point, I guess it'd have to be Rust, the guy I'd wound up choosing as a candidate.

"All the more reason that you should tell us his name, Octavia," King Enoch said.

Yikes, now even Father is getting nosy... Well, if he had a name, I'd totally give it to you, dear Father!

"I cannot tell you his name right now." *That's why I'm in this mess!* "If I told you his name, that would mean I would need to introduce him to you formally. Let me repeat, I do not wish to inconvenience my beloved. Dear Brother...the reason I said what I said was that I merely wanted you to know that information, as a girl and as your little sister."

I had the feeling that was a really good excuse, if I did say so myself. *Okay, so let's just close the matter now! Please?*

"From what you've said...it sounds like your relationship is rather complicated."

N-no, Brother! It's not complicated—it's nonexistent!

I wondered what kind of man he was conjuring up in his head—who in the world was my (fake) boyfriend to him?

"I wish to have some time to speak with your beloved." Sirius nodded thoughtfully. "Whether there's a formal introduction or not, we shall need to set a date, yes? Let me see... Since both of you would need to agree, I suppose tomorrow won't do... So how about ten days...no, two weeks from now. Would that be enough time?"

He was considering asking to meet him tomorrow? *Terrifying.*

And while two weeks *was* a bit longer than ten days, it was still, what, fourteen days? To a well-organized man like my big brother, two weeks would have been more than enough time to arrange something like this...but way too short for me!

There I was, hoping for a good month to find a fake boyfriend to introduce to just Sirius, but now I only had fourteen days? I knew he

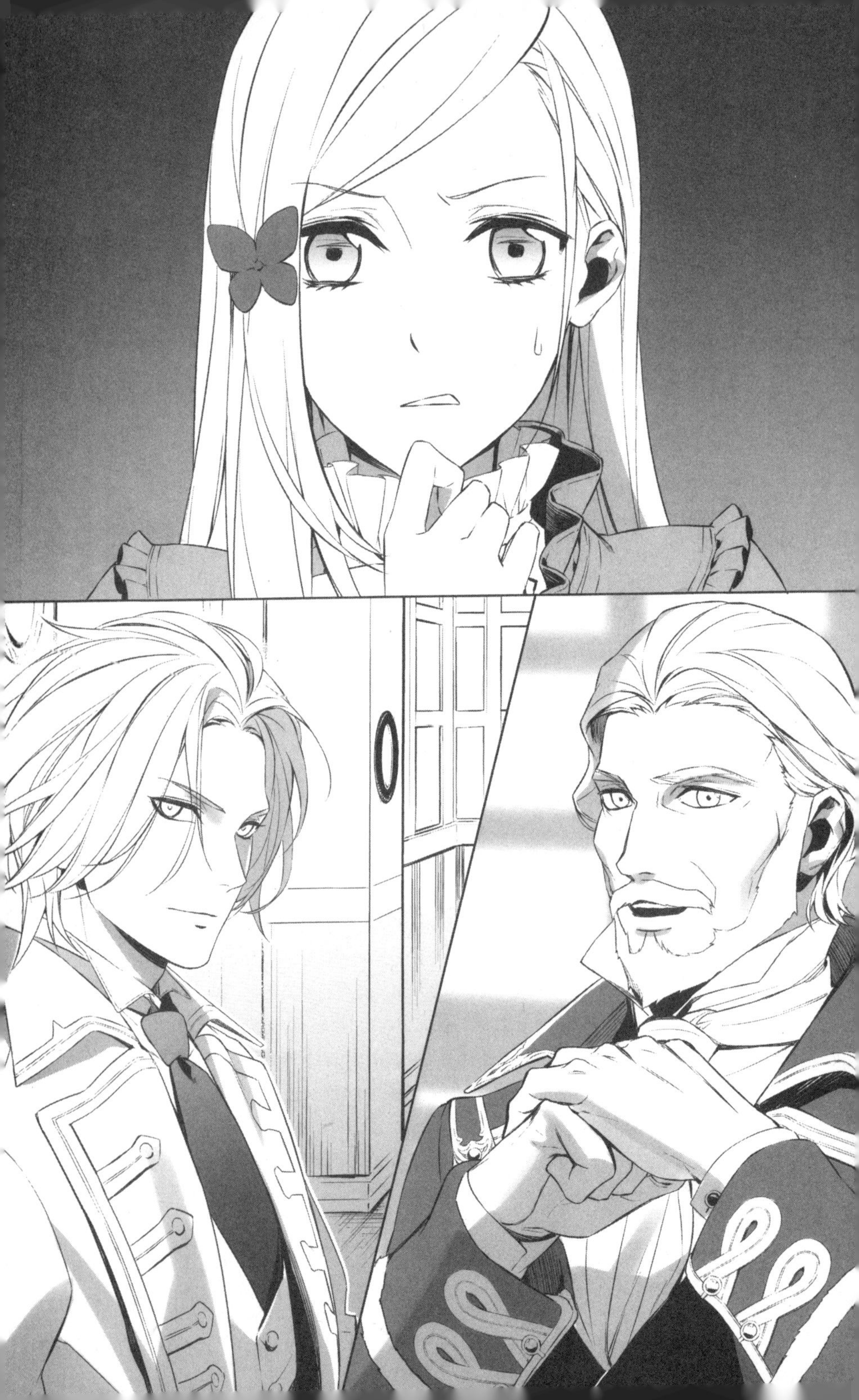

didn't have any malicious intentions—if anything, it was the opposite. But why did he have to go and shorten the time frame like that?!

"Sirius, this is not for you to decide," Father admonished him.

"Yes, but it needs to be done, Father…"

My father sighed heavily, turned to me, and said, "Octavia, come to my office after dinner. I wish to speak with you alone."

"Yes, Father…"

Ugh. What a bummer.

9

And thus, our evening banquet of the day was over. It was a lovely feast—the chefs really outdid themselves this time—but I was unable to taste it halfway through the meal.

I still cleaned my plate, though!

I had the waiter return my fan to me, and I swiftly left the banquet hall. I opened it as I walked and indulged in a moment of sweet escapism.

Ahh, fluffy feathers, I love you so…

But a question snapped me back to reality.

"Your Highness, are you going to go directly to His Majesty's office?" asked a deep, handsome voice.

I stopped in my tracks and turned to face Klifford. Maybe it was because I was now his Sovereign, but Klifford was much more direct with me now. He'd been that way ever since our walk to the banquet hall for dinner. Well, conversations *were* a big first step toward deepening relationships!

"Yes, I suppose so…," I answered.

Stating the obvious here, but Klifford clearly overheard everything that happened at dinner, didn't he? Truth be told, I'd rather go back to my room and catch my breath…and just forget about everything while I'm at it! If you don't wanna do something today, it's always a good idea to put it off until tomorrow!*

But...I couldn't defy a direct order from my father.

I guess I'll have to do as Klifford said and go straight to see Father...

"Dear Sister!"

My face softened into a smile at the sound of the voice. There was only one person who called me dear Sister, and I would never mistake his voice.

"Hi, Alec."

Apparently, Alec had chased after me when I'd left the banquet hall. Alec's bodyguard was at a distance, standing in a corner of the hallway.

"There's something I need to ask you, dear Sister," he said, carefully crafting his sentence. "Your beloved...who is he?"

"Um..." *Well, shit.*

I could just tell Alec the truth, right? No, I want to tell him the truth! Like, I'm dying to tell him! I was able to dodge the matter back at the training grounds, but the situation has clearly taken a turn for the worse.

I wish I could just ask him for advice! But...

I glanced over at Klifford. Our eyes met. He was staring right back at me.

Is it because you're my Adjutant now? We may be able to converse more freely now, but you've been standing a lot closer to me as my bodyguard, eh, Klifford?

At this rate, Klifford was likely to overhear anything I said to Alec, even if I whispered it. And if what I told Alec in confidence—"*What Sirius said pissed me off, so I declared I had a boyfriend who doesn't exist!*"—got out to anyone else, well, that'd be bad.

Don't get me wrong, it's not that I didn't trust Klifford! I just...didn't want my pretentiousness to be exposed...which meant Alec was my only option.

Of course, if I could—if I could!—I'd want to keep Alec in the dark, too, but I was in no position to do that anymore.

Hey, Klifford, can ya take a hint and go away for a few minutes?

I mean, I'm staring right into your eyes!

Hear me! I, your Sovereign, am sending you, my Adjutant, a psychic message!

"......"

"......"

We stared at each other for what felt like an eternity.

W-wait, is this a staring contest? If I look away, do I lose?

He...didn't get the message.

"Dear Sister," Alec said coldly, breaking me out of my lock-eyed gridlock.

Urgh. Yeah, I'd be mad, too. Instead of answering your question, I exhausted myself trying to have a psychic conversation with Klifford.

I turned to Alec.

"I'm sorry, Alec, I didn't mean to ignore you. I just..."

"You just...what?"

"I just...it's not something I can tell you here. Let's set aside some time on another day to talk. I'll come visit you in your room. That should be nice for a change, right?"

"So...this means you have your reasons?"

You're so smart, Alec!

"Why, yes. I do."

Alec exhaled quickly. "All right, then I'll do as you say. I just..."

This time it was Alec's turn to add the *I just* clause.

"I just want, when the time comes...for your bodyguard to not be in the room."

Among royals, it wasn't uncommon for a bodyguard to accompany you to a family member's room—even just to position himself discreetly in the corner of the doorway. Even Sirius would always bring his bodyguard with him whenever he'd come to my room for any reason.

I suppose these were holdovers of an eventful royal family history. It seemed that sometimes vassals were more trustworthy than your own siblings.

But whenever Alec and I visited each other, we'd usually have our bodyguards wait outside the room. If it was just Alec visiting me, it was basically no different than me being in my room alone. I had no need for protection.

So Alec's request here was actually the norm. And based on what I wanted to tell Alec, I definitely had no objections to Alec's request.

Having said that, however...Alec had never been that explicit before.

Yeah, he's definitely wary of Klifford... I guess the whole Turchen thing is the main roadblock here. But that works out perfectly for me, so whatevs. And I can always ask him directly about it when we have our chat later.

"Very well, Alec. I agree."

I actually hadn't set foot much in my father's office before. On both sides of the door to his office stood two soldiers, whose sole job was to guard it. Apparently, they had been told I was coming—as soon as they saw me, they opened the door for me.

I firmly clutched my fan—my steadfast ally—and stepped into my father's office.

The decor was simple and sturdy. It was the complete opposite aesthetic of the royal audience chamber, which was opulently adorned with gold and silver. The king before my father—so, my grandfather—was a jewel collector and a hoarder in general, so I guess it was a reaction to that.

My father was seated at his desk, poring over some documents in hand.

And as for the other people in the room...well, there weren't any. He probably excused everyone else so we could have a private conversation about my boyfriend. Usually, he was accompanied by more than one royal guard.

He set down his documents and looked up at me. "Octavia, welcome."

I curtsied lightly in reply...with a flourish of my opening fan to follow!

Meanwhile...I didn't sense the door close behind me. I could feel the air blowing through the skirt of my dress. *I wonder what those two guards are up to?*

"Ah, good timing. You come in, too," my father called out to someone behind me.

The door was still open. There were three people standing behind me: Klifford and the two soldiers. As for whom my father was specifically addressing—in this case, I'd assume it was Klifford. But I didn't hear Klifford's footsteps. There wasn't a sign of him moving at all! No sign of the door closing, either!

Ah, it's happening again. This is just like earlier when Klifford refused to answer Alec's request for his name. Is it Klifford's policy to only act if I—his Sovereign—command it? Even in a situation like this?!

But the one who'd asked him to come in was my father. The king. He couldn't tease my father by refusing! He was an Adjutant, not an Adju*taunt*!

I looked back at the open door and said, "Klifford, enter."

"Aye," Klifford answered, finally walking into the office.

The guards closed the door completely, positioning Klifford on our side of it—placing him where a bodyguard would normally be posted.

I hid half my face behind my fan, my heart racing as I watched to see what my father would do next.

My father said, "Your bodyguard—he seems to be quite competent."

I think...that's the all clear! Yep, we're safe! Looks like Father interpreted his actions as those of a proper, dutiful guard. Good thing Father took it that way!

"Oh, you mean Klifford? Why, yes, he is."

"You call him by name... Are you two really that intimate?"

"Three months have passed since he was assigned as my bodyguard, Father. Why wouldn't I call him by name?"

I learned his name and said it for the first time just today, but let's not dwell on that!

"That seems like a rather long appointment," Father replied.

And he had a good point. But three months being a "long appointment" was definitely not normal!

Is that why you called Klifford into your office? To root for him?

"Why, yes, it is. And I am most pleased about it," I said, smiling genuinely. I mean, I didn't have to worry anymore about him quitting on me!

And when my father saw his daughter's innocent eyes, shining brightly in a smile, for some reason, he stoically tapped on his desk with the index finger of his left hand.

Um, Father, ain't that a cruel way to react?

"I see..." He brought his right hand to his chin...then he threw a question at me. "Then tell me, Octavia. What would you say if I told you I wanted Klifford to come serve me instead?"

Wha—?! You called Klifford here not to root for him but to uproot him?!

My jaw literally dropped. Though my trusty fan hid that from my father!

"Father...surely you jest? Why, you have many guards whom you consider friends and confidants, do you not? And still you would take Klifford away from me?"

None of my father's guards were in the room at the moment, though...

Incidentally, according to whispers from the chief lady-in-waiting's network of handmaids, one of my father's bodyguards was enduring feelings of unrequited love for him. They weren't physically intimate, but they were in that more-than-friends-less-than-lovers zone... Platonic love? That's called a bromance, right?

Anyway, they were a tightly knit group, and Father had more than enough helping hands.

"I will not let you have Klifford. He is my knight and mine alone."

Nix the changing of the guard for now! I only just now got a commitment from him. I'll never let him go!

But...

I decided to make an addendum.

"Naturally, if you order me as king, that is another matter entirely, and I will comply," I said, smiling this time.

My father was the king, after all. The most powerful person in Esfia. I may have been able to say no to my father, but not to the king.

"So unless I give you my order as king, you will not let him go. Is that correct?"

"Yes, Father." *I thought that was a given.*

"I've heard what you have to say, Octavia…but how does the man in question feel about it?" he asked, lobbing the conversation into Klifford's court. "Answer for Octavia, Alderton."

I looked back at Klifford, wildly staring at him and hoping he'd get the message to answer my father.

Ooh! I may have failed last time, but I think I got through to him this time!

Klifford turned to me and nodded!

"I am deeply honored by your offer, Your Majesty… However, I have made my decision to serve Princess Octavia."

Dang, that was an A-plus answer.

If my father poached Klifford after that line, I'd be shocked.

But, hmm… Wouldn't most people consider serving the king more appealing? Maybe it's because we're Sovereign and Adjutant now.

"When we first spoke of this matter, did you not say it was Octavia's decision to make?"

You…what now? Did Father and Klifford have a talk before?

Come to think of it, Father did use Klifford's full name. I guess it's only natural that he'd keep tabs on his daughter's bodyguard…but something's up.

"As you are well aware, Your Majesty, I come from Turchen. And while Count Alderton adopted me into his house and I am now legally his son, I cannot deny the nature of my lineage. And I have been deeply concerned that this would disgrace you, Your Majesty."

My father lightly shook his head. "Enough… Octavia, Alderton, you've both made your intentions quite clear. Rest assured, I will not demand you two separate."

By the way, Father… I know that the matter of poaching Klifford is closed now. But…I get the feeling that wasn't the reason you called me into your office?

10

I would have loved it if I could have just left then...but of course that wasn't possible. *Sigh...*

"So...was it Klifford you wished to speak with me about? I'd assumed it was about something else."

"Ah, yes...that's right. I asked you in here because I determined that it was necessary to speak with you about the matter Sirius brought up."

I turned my back to Klifford and said, "Klifford...leave us."

He gave me a questioning look, so I nodded at him.

"Yes, Your Highness." Klifford bowed and left the office.

My father sighed heavily after Klifford left his line of sight.

I hated to rehash drama, but I just had to ask him, "Why did you inquire after Klifford?"

He gave me a sarcastic look. "Because unlike you, I can size up a person?"

"Was it...because he is gifted?"

And because he's...an Adjutant? Does my father know about that? Yeah, right. Klifford said I'm the only one who knows... So he can't know, right?

My father neither confirmed nor denied it. "Gifted, you say? Octavia... Regardless of what kind of man he is, you surely have your own opinions of him. But this is my warning to you as your father: Don't let your guard down around Klifford Alderton... That man is poison."

"......" *Whoa there, Father, there's kind of a lot to unpack there! Like, why do you say he's "poison"? Or for that matter, why would you pick a poisonous man to be a knight in the first place?*

"If he is poison, then why did you allow him to be considered for the position of my guard detail?" *Was it just a figure of speech, Dad?*

"It was you who chose him from the group, was it not?"

Oh, right! Ya got me there... I was the one who chose him...by the power of eeny-meeny-miny-moe!

"However…even poison can be medicine if used correctly. So I entrust him to you… We will speak no more of this. Understood, Octavia?"

"Yes, Father…," I said, nodding reluctantly. *With an order like that, we probably really won't talk about Klifford again. I guess that means if I ask him questions about Klifford, he won't give me any answers.*

"Now, let's discuss the matter Sirius brought up—your lover. So…is it true?"

I faltered for a moment, wondering if I should just tell him the truth… But this was also a great opportunity for me to find out how my father felt about my whole marriage situation.

"Yes. I do have a lover," I answered. *Well, I don't, actually! But I'm always on the lookout for one!* I finished in my head with a silent sigh.

I won't speak for my past-life self, but in my current incarnation, I'm pretty good-looking. And to make the most of my natural-born good looks and slender figure I was given as Octavia, I never binge-eat, and I always do some basic exercise. Don't mean to brag, but I'm a real beauty.

So why has a romance or two never fallen into my lap?! It's gotta be the man-on-man romance law of the land… I mean, this entire world was built around Sil and Sirius.

"It would seem that my dear brother suggested a formal introduction for my sake…"

"Do you sincerely think his intentions were good?"

"Were they not?"

For some reason, my father chuckled cynically. "Octavia, you don't need to feign ignorance on my behalf. Sirius said what he did at the dinner table only to see how you would react."

He what now?

"Good intentions or not, my opinion on the matter has not changed," my father said, ignoring my confusion. "It is not my intention to hold you back."

Uh… I don't understand.

"I understand…" I nodded solemnly. I couldn't believe my father had just said that, but I didn't let my confusion show.

"If you are in a loving relationship, then I do not wish to force you two to part."

"Oh...is that so...?"

I'm sorry, Father. I think I had you all wrong. I'd just assumed you were going to force me into a marriage of political convenience...

And as monarch of the kingdom, that would be the correct move. I always thought that maybe he was a little too lenient on Sirius's marriage of love, but parents do have favorites. And try as they might to treat everyone equally, having favorites can make their decisions easier or harder. I mean, parents are people, too!

Also, of course he's gonna love the kid who's more affectionate. I'm a standoffish daughter—and I own it! So I could totally understand if my father was a little standoffish around me, too. Though I can't defend the way he treats Alec!

"So...who is the lucky man?"

"Well..." *Just give him a name! Doesn't matter who... Should I just say it's Rust Byrne? No, I can't, that's not a sure thing...* "I cannot tell you yet." *C-cringe... Stellar answer, Octavia. I don't think I can drag this excuse out much longer.*

"Do you...not trust me?"

"Why, Father, you are considered to be King Eus's second coming. Of course I trust you."

Okay, that should do it.

King Eus was a very famous king in history who helped Esfia develop into the kingdom it is today. He was intelligent, gifted in martial arts, handsome...and apparently, he even smelled great!

"King Eus, eh? Octavia, did you know that before Eus became king, his elder sister reigned for a month?"

I made a strange face in my mind. *Well, that's odd...*

Since I loved BL light novels in my past life, even after I was reborn as Octavia, I still craved them in print. I mean, I retained my consciousness as Maki Tazawa—of course my tastes were going to stay the same.

In other words, I craved BL light novels! But of course, I couldn't find any. And I know you're probably thinking, why do you need BL light novels when you're surrounded by the real thing?

I would almost agree with you that it's illogical...but I actually do have a logical reason for feeling this way. I mean, 2D is just completely different from 3D! With everything in 3D, my little *fujoshi* heart simply cannot satisfy its 2D cravings!

I went through a phase where I slaved away trying to write my own... but that didn't work. I just didn't want to write my own stories! I wanted to read BL light novels written by somebody else!

So I eventually settled on the diaries of Esfian men in the libraries. I pored over their passionate accounts of "friendship" between men to exercise my fantasy muscles... But I finished reading everything too soon. There just weren't that many stories to read.

After that, I moved on to reading Esfia's history so I could learn more about the royal family that I belonged to. And it was there that I read about King Eus! He even had a biography written about him: *The Legend of King Eus*. And lemme tell you, that book spun some serious tales of loyalty, friendship, and betrayal between men—it was actually pretty decent for a *fujoshi* like me! It gave my fangirling fantasy brain quite the rush. That biography was actually how I learned that King Eus smelled good. His vassals wrote about it for posterity!

However...

I searched my memory. I didn't remember any account of King Eus's elder sister. She didn't even get a mention in his biography.

"I suppose you wouldn't have heard of her... She was Esfia's final female queen, and she was expunged from the records. Nobody even knows her name."

"Did King Eus...have her assassinated?"

That's the only conclusion I could draw. But King Eus? Say it ain't so! There weren't any illustrations of him, but in the biography, he was described as a wonderful and handsome man—in my mind, I'd dreamed him up into the most fangirlable guy in the book!

"Yes, he did," my father confirmed, unfortunately.

I pressed my fan to my lips and heaved a disappointed sigh. I probably had a very perplexed look on my face.

"But King Eus thought the world of his sister...and he was overjoyed by her enthronement. She was a very wise queen, too. People had faith that she could be the one to break the cycle of Esfia's ominous history."

The cycle of Esfia's ominous history?

"In all of Esfia's history—what we know of it, at least—there were four female queens, including Eus's sister. And each of their reigns was cut short by an unnatural death. The kingdom was in chaos. The people had hoped that King Eus's sister could free Esfia from such a turbulent past."

There were four whole queens? I always assumed Esfia was only ruled by men...

"Could it be that King Eus's sister was a corrupt ruler...and that's why he had her assassinated?"

"Eus's sister's wise governance angered the Sky God, so He had her assassinated. That's what's written in the records that only Esfia's royal family can read."

The Sky God... Up until then, I hadn't really given this world's deity a passing thought.

But..."God"...huh?

"You were just unlucky."

The words I heard in my final moments as Maki Tazawa entered my mind.

"Well, the Sky God isn't always in the right," I said quickly, locking the bad memories deep in my mind before they could resurface.

"Don't blaspheme our God, Octavia."

"Forgive me...," I said, quickly bowing my head. "Please forget I said that, Father."

Yep. Bad memories are terrible for your mental health—let's lock 'em up.

"Octavia, don't misunderstand me. I am envious of you, actually."

I looked up. There was a slightly self-deprecating smile on my father's lips.

"Father…?"

"I succumbed to it, you see," he said in a half sigh. Then he looked back at me. His eyes were solemn. "Octavia…do you want to become queen?" he asked.

"No," I answered quickly. Well, I meant it!

In terms of aptitude, Sirius was fine for the task, and taking *The Noble King* into consideration, it also made sense that he would be the next king. Though, if I had my way, I'd have Alec become king…

But I'm just not cut out for being a queen. Big nope! I already have my hands full being a princess!

My father smirked at me. "I suppose that's the only way you could answer. And I shouldn't have pried, either. Forgive me for the foolish question. Forget I asked it."

"All right…I'll forget it."

"It's just…there are whispers—many whispers—that you are aiming for the throne."

That I'm…what now? So that's why he asked me that question? Geez, it's just been one surprise after another ever since I set foot in this office!

"It's made Sirius more vigilant than he needs to be. He worries that Sil will be harmed by all of this, you see. And as long as there are no skeletons in your closet, then I see no problem with giving your beloved a formal introduction."

So I can't avoid the formal introduction thing…? There's something about the way Father is talking, though…

"Earlier, you said you did not wish to separate us…but were you sincere? Do I really have your blessing to have a romance with a gentleman of my choice?"

That is, Father, "Are ya gonna let me marry for love?" Let's get a yes or no statement, loud and clear!

"Unless I know the gentleman in question, I cannot give my judgment. But I certainly won't refuse outright."

Su-weeeet! If anything, this just gave me a big opportunity! The I Have a Boyfriend train chugs on! And then, if we break up, I'll be a free woman!

It sure was smart of me to avoid the collision with the Pre-Ordained Marriage of Convenience express!

"There is an exception, however."

Lemme guess, the kind of guy who'd get immediately rejected if I brought him home... So a guy who's on really bad terms with the royal family or, like, a violent criminal? I wonder what permissible range we're looking at in terms of social class? I'd better get some detailed intel now while I can! Which qualities are a no go?!

"An exception? And what sort of gentleman would that be?"

"If you tell me now who your beloved is, then I'll explain."

You said that knowing I can't tell you, you dirty rat!

My father and I smiled sweetly at each other.

Then my father's smile vanished, and he said, "You can't be persuaded to give me his name right now?"

"No, Father. Please forgive me. I promise I'll bring him to the reception that Brother proposed in two weeks' time."

I'd rather have a month, but I'll make that concession and go for two weeks like Sirius said.

Two weeks! I only have two weeks to secure a (fake) boyfriend and bring him home to meet my family. Then we'll probably shift over to the engagement period. So I guess that gives me a year total?

And during that year, I've gotta snag me a true love! I'll just make up some excuse, like I had a change of heart, so I can break up amicably with my (fake) boyfriend and get on the Marry My True Love express!

That's the move! Let's make some lemonade out of these lemons!

And thus, it was decided that I would bring my (fake) boyfriend home to meet the family in two weeks' time.

Just as I was about to let my wave of relief carry me out of the office, my father stopped me.

"Octavia, wait. An invitation has arrived for you from House Reddington."

"From Countess Reddington?"

"She wants to invite you to her junior ball two days from now."

Only the king could hold a ball. All other nobles held junior balls. Esfia made this distinction very clear. Naturally, all balls were held at the royal castle. So even if I didn't attend any junior balls, there would be no social repercussions, as long as I attended the proper balls here. However, it was a little unusual for somebody to invite a guest to either type of ball just two days prior.

"My, what a rushed invitation," I said.

"It seems there were some issues on her end. She probably wants you there as her centerpiece. Your appearance at these sorts of social functions is rare, after all."

Rosa Reddington was one of the few noblewomen in Esfia who held any appreciable amount of power. She was a countess and thirty-five years old. She and I had spoken many times at public gatherings. So if I had to say...I guess we were friends?

The junior ball, eh...? I've been diligently ditching this sort of social function my whole life!

In my defense, Esfia's junior balls were far from typical. You'd eat, dance, and socialize there. Boys and girls would dance together, too. That much was typical.

But...boys would also dance with boys! It was a place where many boys found their Prince Charmings.

Only in Esfia, amirite?

At first, the *fujoshi* in me really enjoyed attending the balls to people-watch. But I'm a hopeless romantic, too, you know! There I was, no signs of romance on my horizon, being forced to watch all the boys become couples left and right, year after year... It's torture for a teenage girl! I know all too well how my eyes were glazing over like a dead fish, just like my handmaids.

Which was why every time an invitation came from some noble family, I'd attend only when absolutely necessary, and I'd ditch the rest.

But that would all end today. I made the decision to attend as many social events as possible to find a boyfriend.

"What sorts of people do you suppose will attend?" I asked.

Although, seeing as how it's mostly gonna be nobles on my big brother's side, maybe I shouldn't get my hopes up.

My father reached out and silently handed me the invitation. I took it and glanced over it. There was a short, polite letter to me, followed by the names of all the attendees.

Hmm... Neither of the leaders of the two main factions of Esfia are on the list. And I don't see very many influential noblemen on here, either... Oh, wait!

There was my man! There were the glittering letters, dancing on the paper: Duke Nightfellow! It looked like his eldest son—Derek Nightfellow—was on the list right after him. Derek was a friend of Sirius, so asking him to be my (fake) boyfriend would be a no go...but I'd get to meet his father!

That was enough to get my heart to lean more in favor of attending. Then...I saw it. My eyes stopped on a name I'd almost overlooked: Rust Byrne.

Looks like I won't need to wait for the letter from Heller after all.

That settled it. "Father, tell Countess Reddington that I gladly accept her invitation."

A Secret Conversation Between Sirius and Derek

Late that night, when I saw my friend show up in the secret passageway to speak with me, I sighed. I could tell just from the look on his face what his answer to my query was.

Not again...

I slumped heavily into my chair. "So the culprit named Octavia again, did he?"

"I'm afraid so...," my friend Derek Nightfellow said, drawing his chin in. "If anything, this makes the whole thing seem contrived. That the men who tried to kill Sil all uniformly named Octavia as their mastermind. It's clearly a fabrication." Derek scratched his head and shook it softly.

"Or...what if it's the truth?"

"Sirius! Don't—"

"I want to pursue every lead we have, that's all. And if there's any suspicion, we should not remove my little sister from the list of suspects. Even if it's not Octavia herself...then could it be this 'beloved' she keeps talking about? If he even is her beloved..."

"That's the theory you favor? I heard the rumors; I wouldn't think it odd if Princess Octavia had a lover. You and Sil are in love, after all."

I argued, "But don't you find it even odder that we haven't heard a peep of gossip about the princess's secret love all this time? As if nobody would know. But his face? His name? Nobody in this castle knows a thing about him."

"But if anyone could keep such a secret, wouldn't it be Princess Octavia? You know she could hide it flawlessly."

I know my little sister. Derek's right; she could keep any secret. That wouldn't surprise me. However...

"There's a possibility that this mystery man does exist...," I said. "But instead of her beloved, he's her collaborator."

"Even if that were true, then why would she go out of her way to tell you she has a beloved? She could just stay quiet."

"It might have been Octavia's personal way of declaring war."

Derek looked up at the ceiling with a frustrated sigh. "If she gave us any other reason to suspect her, I would agree with you...but I think you're just overanalyzing things. The assassins simply took advantage of the already existing rumors about her and used her name. That's all. The name of Princess Octavia makes a great cloak of invisibility simply by invoking it."

If you need proof, just look at how confused you are was what he was probably thinking.

All of the people in my circle tended to be wary of Octavia. The only exceptions were Sil—the love of my life—and Derek.

"Why do you stick up for Octavia so? Is it because of Duke Nightfellow?"

While he didn't exert his authority publicly, beneath the surface, Duke Nightfellow wielded massive amounts of influence... And for some reason, Octavia took a liking to him. He doted on her like a daughter in turn. And Derek was the duke's eldest son. He got his brown eyes and hair from his mother, but his face and personality resembled his father.

"My father and Princess Octavia may be friendly, but I haven't spoken with her much over the past few years. In fact, I used to torment her out of spite, since my father was strict with me but always indulged her."

"Oh…is that so?"

For a moment, there was a strange look in Derek's eyes. "Yes… But I overcame my spite when you and Father found out and gave me a thrashing for it. And if anything, due to those terrifying memories, I've had a bit of an Octavia phobia for the past few years and…"

Derek trailed off midsentence. "Sirius," he said. "What are your feelings for Octavia? Tell me."

What are my feelings for Octavia? That's easy.

"Ever since we were young…I've disliked her."

And it was pretty clear that the feeling was mutual. My little sister hated me, ever since we were little. Kindness begets kindness. Animosity begets animosity. But the world in which we lived was not that simple. If I couldn't put Octavia's animosity toward me behind us, then I was unfit to be king. But things never went well for me when it came to Octavia.

"Ever since you were young?" Derek sounded confused.

"What?"

"Have you forgotten? How you used to be so…"

So?

"What?"

"So the opposite. When Princess Octavia treated you spitefully, you always tried to win her favor. You told me you loved her so much you couldn't help yourself… That you would dote on her, even if she hated it. You loved her greatly."

"I…loved Octavia?" Not even speaking the words aloud made me believe them.

"Come, come now, have you truly forgotten? When I tormented her as a child, it wasn't only because of my father. It was because I didn't like the way she treated you, too. Don't you remember what you did when I pushed Octavia to the ground?"

"What…I did?"

"You erupted and got into a punching and cursing match with me. Princess Octavia had to get your father to come stop us. I was scolded severely for it."

"Surely you jest...?"

If I had witnessed Derek pushing my sister, I would have rebuked him, yes...but would I have flown into a violent rage on behalf of my sister...? Inconceivable.

"You took the words from my mouth, Sirius. If you doubt me, then ask your father. When did you forget? *Why* did you forget? Don't you remember anything from that day?"

I was about to answer no...when a silhouette appeared in my mind.

"＿＿ ＿＿ ＿＿ ＿＿＿＿..."

But like a haze, the vision quickly disappeared.

"Sirius...?"

"R-right." I shook my head. "It was a vision from when I was a young boy... I suppose the memory does get vague now and then. But even if I did try to become friendly with Octavia when we were young, I am no longer that little boy. It's as simple as that. And ensuring Sil's safety is far more important to me now. This all started three months ago now."

Someone was trying to murder Sil. We had thought the threat was neutralized when the mastermind behind the plot was killed. But starting three months ago, the attempts on Sil's life had resumed.

As for the motive...we did not know. We still had no grasp on who the mastermind was. I was always one step behind.

Until one day, we caught the assassin—a man who was probably just a pawn—and he gave us the name of his master...Octavia.

The second assassin we caught many days ago said the same thing.

We couldn't take them at face value. In my head, I knew that. The assassins might have been lying. Perhaps someone instructed them to lie. But did that really prove Octavia's innocence?

"Three months ago... Wait, are you saying you think Princess Octavia's bodyguard is the prime suspect?"

"It's Klifford Alderton. The attempts on Sil's life started after he came here."

"But he hasn't behaved suspiciously at all," Derek argued. "And please stop trying to say that his obsessive protection of Princess Octavia is grounds for suspicion. Remember what Sil said? He resembles the man who saved his life four years ago. If they are one and the same, he would be our ally, in fact."

"You are far too optimistic."

Our ally? The Emissary of Ongarne is our ally?

I restrained myself from saying that. That wasn't the sort of thing I should say out loud—not even around Derek.

I was certain that Father knew of that man's true nature, but he didn't inform me himself. I found out another way. And I must suppress the information I discovered. But it was difficult to approach Alderton himself when he was Octavia's bodyguard.

The Emissary of Ongarne—he was the man who slaughtered Nathaniel, rebel to the royal family and the reigning leader of the Saza Church. The mastermind behind the attempts on Sil's life *was* Nathaniel. Unfortunately, we'd never be able to question Nathaniel and find out why he'd wanted to murder Sil.

The attempts on Sil's life should have ended with Nathaniel's death. But someone out there was still trying to eliminate Sil. And could we really say with confidence that it wasn't Octavia?

What if Octavia and Klifford Alderton—the Emissary of Ongarne—hadn't met three months ago? What if they had a connection before then? Wouldn't that add new insights into Nathaniel's assassination plot?

There were rumors that Octavia was contemplating her coronation as queen. Ordinarily, if anyone were to be named as my rival heir, it would be Alexis. But the fact of the matter was, rumors of Octavia desiring the throne were far more believable.

If Octavia had laid the groundwork for this plot—or if someone was just making it look that way—then my father's feelings were almost certainly related. Father wanted to revoke Alexis's right of succession. The only thing that was holding him back were the many voices of dissent from the nobility at the time—he knew that if he tried to force the matter, the dissent might escalate into full-on war. When my father walked back his intentions, the issue was settled privately.

But the fact that Father had no intention of giving the throne to Alexis was well-known among the nobility. This was an uncharacteristically careless act for King Enoch *because* the circumstances of Alexis's birth had angered him so.

If all of this was true, that is.

Father neglected Alexis because he was the product of one night's mistake. But was that really true?

That was probably why there were more whispers of the possibility of Octavia being crowned, rather than Alexis. The successor to the throne was to be chosen by the current king—our father. And even though Alexis had a claim to the throne, he hadn't set any wheels in motion to make this happen. And the nobles, knowing this—and knowing Octavia's reputation—fanned the flames until the rumors grew into what they were today.

Naturally, there was a way for Alexis to ascend to the throne. If he raised an army and staged a coup against Father, that would be another matter entirely. However…was that what Alexis really wanted?

Then what about Octavia? Father never once mentioned her claim to the throne. At the very least, he never said she was deprived of it. There was still the possibility he could name her. Rather, he left that possibility open.

If I were to die, it would be Octavia, not Alexis, who would ascend to the throne. If Octavia herself had shown any indication that the rumors were true, this would all have been much easier. But her actions were never outside the scope of what was normal for a princess.

If my little sister did have ambitions, however—if she saw me as an enemy standing in her way to the throne—then she would surely target my weakness. And my weakness was Sil. If I were to lose Sil, I would be as good as dead. She had no need to lay a single finger on me. As a target…that was her most strategic move.

As I stood there in silence, Derek continued, "How do you explain the fact that Sil has been saved numerous times because of Princess Octavia? Don't tell me you've forgotten."

"I…haven't forgotten."

My relationship with Octavia was never good. Octavia had never approved of my relationship with Sil, either. But despite this, she *had* given me advice that led to saving Sil from danger. And most of this happened *after* the threat of Nathaniel had disappeared. She helped bring to light a few insiders who—though they didn't actively plot to kill him—were extremely hostile toward Sil.

She knew so much that it frightened me... Her predictions were both accurate and detailed—almost as if our lives were a story she had read in a book once.

"Octavia knows too much," I argued. "How did she gather all her intelligence?"

"Perhaps she's hired a good spy."

"Then explain why she stopped giving me advice three months ago?"

Derek sighed melodramatically. "It seems that you insist on suspecting Princess Octavia is the mastermind, eh, Sirius?"

And it seems you insist on assuming she's innocent. It's just too contrived.

"It struck me as odd that she refused to name this lover of hers at the dinner table," I said.

"Is that why you suggested a formal introduction?" Derek asked. "As a ploy to draw him out? Thanks to those blabbering dinner servants, everyone in the castle knows about it already."

"Good."

"And what will you do if he turns out to actually be her lover?"

"Then...I'll give him my blessing." *As a brother should.*

"Then you'll push Princess Octavia into marriage...and when she gives birth, you'll take her child to raise as your own?" Derek asked in an almost teasing tone.

"You wish to lecture me about my heir, too? I hadn't really given it much thought. However..."

It was true. I hadn't thought about it...much...

"However?"

"If it were possible...," I whispered, my voice disappearing into the back of my throat.

After a pause, Derek continued, "You actually said yes... I didn't think you would."

Sirius...you really have forgotten, haven't you?

The next morning, I was informed that Octavia would formally introduce her beloved to the family in thirteen days' time.

The World Through the Emissary of Ongarne's Eyes: 1

The royal castle changed its appearance with the rising and setting of the sun.

"If you please, Sir Alderton." The chief lady-in-waiting bowed and placed her hand on the door.

It was the end of day. At this time, the door to the princess's bedchamber was locked from the outside. Her bodyguard, Klifford, was not permitted to go near, and Octavia herself was not allowed to leave her room until the morning. And her bedchamber was not the only room that was locked. The nearby castle grounds were completely closed off, with the princess alone inside. It was very thorough.

To say it was for Octavia's safety would be the charitable way of putting it. But it was a beautiful prison no one could enter… That would be a more apt way of describing it.

Octavia's movement was always restricted. A bodyguard was by her immediate side during the day, and aside from the time spent alone in her bedchamber, there were always many people in her vicinity. She spent her nights locked up like this.

Esfia's royal family was blessed by the Sky God—though in Klifford's view, they were cursed. While their reign was patriarchal, their bloodline was passed down through their princesses.

Long ago, there was a princess who despaired her fate and escaped. She was the king of Esfia's daughter. Her family searched for her in a frenzy and returned her to the castle. That was why Esfia's royal line continued to be the superpower it was without faltering until the present day.

It was quite the distorted kingdom. Kings and princes mated with men—they did not pass on their own blood.

Klifford amended his last thought: No, they *could not* pass on their own blood. King Enoch, who sired Alexis himself, was the one exception.

Consequently, every generation had a princess who produced an heir. To Esfia, princesses were treasures to be protected.

There were also those who opposed this system. Was it not *because* they had princesses that the royal men—the kings—could take husbands and abandon their reproductive responsibilities? If the continuing homosexual marriages resulted in the collapse of their bloodline, would that not correct the distortion?

The castle echoed especially loudly at night. As the chief lady-in-waiting locked the door, the abrasive sound of the metal keys rubbing against each other rang out.

"Sir Alderton," she called to him.

Klifford redirected his gaze from the door to the chief lady-in-waiting. She was leaning her back against the door, keys in hand, with a troubled look on her face.

"How much longer do you suppose this will go on?" she asked. "Princess Octavia hasn't expressed any discontent outright, but as much as this is to protect her, I simply can't—"

"Only until matters settle down," Klifford replied coolly. "That is what His Majesty has instructed."

The kings of yore always placed their princesses under strict protection and surveillance. But it was three months ago that Enoch had started locking Octavia in her beautiful prison at night. In no small way was this also to keep an eye on her, but it was first and foremost a strict measure to ensure his daughter's safety. The latter implication was much stronger.

To fight back against the forces who sought to assassinate the one princess and destroy the system. Isolating Octavia was the quickest way to ensure her protection from those whom he suspected might harm her...even from Klifford, her bodyguard.

The words King Enoch told him the day he was chosen as Octavia's bodyguard appeared in his mind: *"I do hope you have no intentions of destroying my treasure...Ongarne."*

"I do not understand what you mean, Your Majesty," Klifford had replied.

"If the treasure is destroyed, the winds of change will no doubt blow through the halls of my family home. However, I do not wish for my treasure to be destroyed. Heed me well; this is an order."

"Order or no, Your Majesty, I have only just had the great honor of being chosen as Princess Octavia's bodyguard."

"Don't make me laugh...Ongarne. You were indeed chosen—but do you really mean to serve Octavia as her bodyguard? I know you did not wish it."

"I suppose...that is for Princess Octavia to decide, Your Majesty."

"Sir Alderton...," the chief lady-in-waiting finally murmured after Klifford's answer. "Little good it does for me to say this, but please take good care of Princess Octavia."

Klifford walked through the dimly lit castle. After his daily duties were finished, he had to walk down the Great Corridor from Octavia's bedchamber to the room he was given as her bodyguard. Apparently, this was an honor reserved for bodyguards.

As always, he and the corridor guard exchanged glances, and after going through the prescribed formalities, he entered the Great Corridor. But the moment he entered, he sensed an irregularity in the air... He wasn't alone.

The unexpected guest was standing in the center of the corridor, gazing up at the painting on the ceiling. It was a painting depicting the creation myth of the Sky God—a tale of mercy and wrath.

For a moment, Klifford gazed up at the majestic ceiling from where he stood. The ceiling was well lit, so the divine resplendence of the creation myth shone best at night. However, given the royal family's bloody history, Klifford found this sanctimonious Great Corridor to be the most abrasive space in the castle.

A corridor to worship the Sky God, of all things...

Klifford walked the corridor in silence. Perhaps this visitor had been waiting for him. On the stone floor, beneath the Sky God's watch, were paintings of heinous wars on Earth. Esfia's second prince, Alexis, stood at its center.

"Alderton," he said. "Who the hell are you, really?"

"You already know the answer, Your Highness. I am Klifford Alderton."

Esfia's second prince was good friends with his sister. This was a fact known by all. However...

"Then tell me, what are you to my sister?"

"Her bodyguard. That is the only answer I can give." But as he answered, he recalled being invited into the defenseless princess's bedchamber.

And the moment he gave Octavia his Insignia... The first time she called him Klifford, his emotions stirred.

"My Sovereign."

He was tempted to laugh at the irony of it all. To think that he would once again gain a Sovereign—something he'd so adamantly neglected—and by his own will, no less.

"Well, I can't trust a bastard like you," Alexis said.

That's right. You shouldn't trust me, Klifford thought.

Octavia, the one who'd so brazenly told him the opposite, was the strange one. And it also made her worthy of being his Sovereign.

"Resign from your post as my sister's bodyguard at once."

"Tell me...did you give this same order to all of Princess Octavia's former bodyguards?"

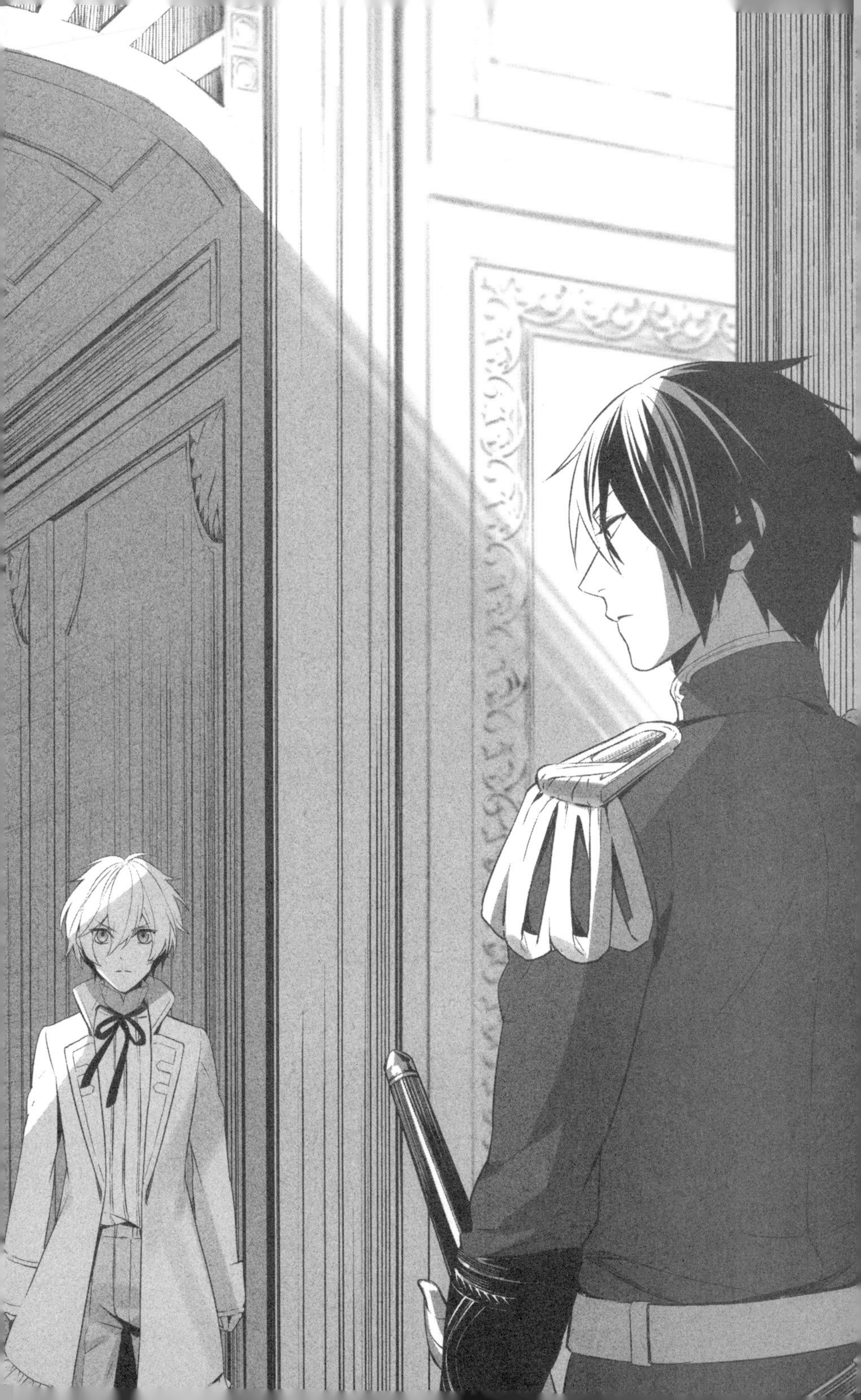

Alexis's brow furrowed.

"Princess Octavia's bodyguards changed quite frequently until now. Prince Alexis...were you somehow involved in that?"

"What a stupid question," Alexis spat, shaking his head. "I feel no need to answer that. You shouldn't be near my sister. That much is clear."

He's absolutely right. However... "So? What's your point?"

Alexis shot an icy glare at Klifford—it was a look he had surely never shown Octavia before.

Klifford brushed it off and said, "Don't forget that Princess Octavia is the only person who can command me. She herself wished me to be her bodyguard. If she commands me to retire, then I shall obey."

"If my sister wished it...," he murmured spitefully. Then he suddenly looked up. There was a mocking glint in the second prince's eyes. "Do you mean to...compensate my sister for her trust?"

"I will do whatever Princess Octavia wishes of me," he said sincerely. He would slaughter Octavia's—his Sovereign's—enemies and protect her as her loyal Adjutant. There were no falsehoods in his words.

Not yet... Wait until the time comes.

"If you betray my sister, I'll end your life myself."

"I'd like to see you try."

"Why, you—!" Alexis was about to speak when the door to the Great Corridor opened.

"Prince Alexis! Please do not wander off alone—not even to the Great Corridor!"

It was one of his bodyguards. The man's eyes widened when he saw Klifford. He was a new recruit. Though Octavia was infamous for perpetually changing bodyguards, Alexis's bodyguards rarely served him for long periods of time, either.

Alexis sighed. "Don't make a fuss—sometimes I just feel like coming here. But no matter, I'm done. I'm going back to my bedchamber."

"Allow me to escort you, Your Highness."

"Fine..."

As Alexis turned and walked away with his bodyguard in tow, Klifford called out, "Prince Alexis...do you like the Great Corridor?"

Alexis gave him a dubious look. "So what if I do?"

"Then that is very true to form."

"......"

Alexis stared back emotionlessly—it was difficult to tell how he took it. Then he left the Great Corridor. His bodyguard and Klifford exchanged nods.

When the Great Corridor was once again filled with solemn silence, Klifford looked up at the painting on the ceiling for the first time in a great while...the painting that filled him with such revulsion.

11

When one RSVPs yes to a junior ball, one must get ready for it!

The junior ball was to be held at its usual location. There were several well-appointed rental halls in the royal capital, and most wealthy nobles utilized them.

Naturally, it was also acceptable to use your own mansion to hold a junior ball. In exchange, however, you needed to provide your own catering, servants to handle your invited guests, a musical selection and an orchestra to play the music—all accommodations had to be done by yourself. Some people attempted to host junior balls...only to fail epically.

If your ball was a success, you got a big status boost—that was a huge plus. But being a host required a lot of time and effort—that was a huge minus. It was also a major time sink. The main types who chose to throw a ball were nobles who were high in rank but low in wealth or families who wanted to fix their bad reputations in one big bang... Most families probably opted out.

Thus, the rental hall. While the rental fee was high, it came with everything included. If you wanted your banquet hall to look cute, you needed only to make a request, and your banquet hall would come embellished with hundreds of ribbons. If you requested a unique menu, dishes from foreign lands would be served. It meant that with the right ideas and the right price, you could throw the ball of your dreams with very little time or effort.

Countess Reddington was to hold her ball at one of those rental halls. It was called Paradise in the Sky, and it was the most popular among the nobility. The *Sky* part of the name was a reference to the Sky God, naturally. And it had only the best-quality furnishings to reflect this.

The *Paradise* part of the name was inspired by its beautiful garden. The garden was a great place to slip out to and admire the flowers when you needed a little break. It was also a great place for couples to retreat hand in hand for secret trysts.

It took about one hour by carriage to get to Paradise in the Sky from the royal castle. So I wouldn't have to worry about losing a day to travel. I would arrive in plenty of time if I left the castle on the day of.

My biggest issue was...my party dress!

What should I wear to the ball? To be exact, my dress, shoes, and jewelry! To call this combination the Holy Trinity would not be an exaggeration. They were a lady's combat uniform! This is how it is!

An esteemed princess must adorn herself accordingly when she makes public appearances! You see, ordinarily, I wear super-comfy dresses that I can easily get in and out of myself. I mean, it serves me well for political matters, too, and I like to wear muted designs so I won't stick out like a sore thumb when I walk around the castle...but at a junior ball, none of that would do.

I needed to go all out and dress up.

To that end, my chief lady-in-waiting came to fetch me first thing in the morning and took me to the costume room. I was there to choose not only my dress but the entirety of my combat uniform. Everything in my usual schedule was changed.

"I can't believe you're attending a junior ball, Your Highness... Ooh, my fingers are itching to play dress-up! Don't you worry, your Matilda has a good grasp on the current trends."

Matilda was the name of my chief lady-in-waiting. She was the daughter of a baron who had, despite her occasional dead-fish eyes, climbed up the ladder to attain her position. When we first met, she was still a mere handmaid. Now she was a thirty-six-year-old spinster. But she looked to be in her twenties. She was a black-eyed, black-haired beauty with a mole under her left eye.

Actually, I heard that after Matilda turned thirty, there were many talks of her getting married. But she swatted all her suitors away.

"I'm already over the hill anyway... And I wish to make this castle my final resting place. I have chosen to wed my career as chief lady-in-waiting."

Swoon.

In fact, becoming a chief lady-in-waiting was tantamount to winning the retirement jackpot. When it was time to retire, you received a pension, and even your own plot of land if you wished. There were lots of benefits to be gained along the way, too. So even without a husband, you were guaranteed a good life in your golden years.

Since same-sex romance was the norm in the royal capital among the upper-class, a simple marriage of love between a man and a woman was quite difficult. But surprisingly enough, there were paths for women to live well even without marriage. It's ironic, really.

Meanwhile, outside the royal capital, the chance of a man being your romantic rival was low, but it was difficult for women to support themselves independently with a career. Each lifestyle had its pros and cons.

"Sorry for the wait, Your Highness," Matilda said, arriving with several dresses that had been hanging in the costume room's giant closet. Every year, I ordered a new party dress for formal occasions. I also had my measurements taken. That was one way to amass a huge dress collection without realizing it...

It was a system set in place to avoid the trap of having nothing to wear when you needed it the most. Being able to respond to any sort of news in the blink of an eye—that was the costume room's role. Once you had a good collection of all the basics, a handmaid could easily make the necessary alterations.

There were dresses I'd only worn once, and at a glance, the practice seemed wasteful. But a princess simply couldn't be seen in the same dress more than once, or in cheap clothing.

"These are all the current trends. Showing a little skin is the most recent craze. The popular colors are red and green. And black is also a color to keep your eye on."

I set my fan down on the desk and took a good moment to look over each dress Matilda brought for me. I even touched the fabrics.

Each dress was designed to show a lot of cleavage. None of them covered the shoulders, either. The colors were either dark red or green. Primary colors. *Yuck. The design and the colors are rubbing me the wrong way... You call this fashion?!*

"Lady Matilda, Her Highness does not follow trends. Could we perhaps prioritize her preferences?"

My handmaid Sasha, who'd walked in with Matilda, brought three dresses forward that were just my type. Not only were they proper party wear, but each was comfortable and easy to move in. Each had sleeves and covered the chest and shoulder areas. They were in muted pastel colors. *That's my Sasha!*

"I see what you mean...," Matilda murmured, hand to her cheek. "Her Highness's preferences are the complete opposite of what's popular."

Ordinarily, I'd pounce on any suggestion Sasha made. However...

"Are there perhaps any dresses...in between what you two chose? I wish for a dress that combines the assets of both styles."

Fashionable yet not betraying my own style. *I remember a saying from my former life in Japan that goes, "He who hunts two hares catches none"...but I'm gonna prove 'em wrong and catch me two hares, baby!*

Matilda and Sasha's eyes widened. Matilda's jaw had dropped, too.

"I'd considered your attending the junior ball in the first place to be a rarity already...but to hear you make such a suggestion of your own volition... You truly are keen, aren't you, Your Highness?"

Hell yeah, I am!

"Well, I have a feeling it's going to be a very special junior ball. I simply wish to enter the fray wearing a dress that's perfect for me."

Just between you and me, right after breakfast and before Matilda came to fetch me this morning, I'd received a letter from Heller. Ordinarily, I would never be able to receive a letter from a common soldier—even if he was a member of the nobility—but as long as I knew a letter was coming beforehand, I had a way around that.

According to Heller's letter, he contacted Rust right away and received a reply that said, in effect, that he would indeed be attending Countess Reddington's junior ball. And though Heller carefully wrote all the details in the letter, basically, the gist of it was: "If you want to meet Rust, go to the junior ball." Just like I figured it would say!

From what I knew about Rust as a character in *The Noble King*, this was a rather authentic method for him. How Rust, a man who was supposed to be in hiding, would be able to go unnoticed while on Countess Reddington's official guest list remained a mystery. Perhaps it had something to do with the abrupt way the countess invited me...

Anyway, my face-to-face meeting with Rust was good to go. And now he knew that I wanted to meet him.

I need to make a good impression on Rust. First impressions are everything, after all!

In response to my eager request, Matilda and Sasha carefully selected dresses for me. Matilda chose a deep green dress with aquamarine accents. Its design was bold yet elegant. It showed only a little skin. I thought it was pretty grown-up.

And Sasha chose a pale blue dress—the same color as my eyes. The skirt had two layers, and it was adorned with lace and ribbons. It felt a bit conservative, but the design boldly emphasized the bust and back. The level of skin exposure on Sasha's dress also felt quite grown-up.

Both dresses suited my personal style and fit the current fashion trends. That's my Matilda and Sasha!

"You both did splendidly. Thank you."

Matilda bowed. "I am deeply humbled, Your Highness."

"So...which dress do you prefer, Your Highness?" Sasha asked, her eyes full of anticipation.

Hmm... It's so difficult to decide. Especially since I don't know what Rust likes... I'd at least like to get a man's opinion.

Alec...is probably deep in his studies right now. I don't want to bother him... Yeah, yeah, I know, my baby brother is the only person I can depend on in times like this! And though Alec is definitely a guy... He's a guy, but...he's just my baby brother...!

A man...

A lightbulb went off in my brain.

But I do have a man! My bodyguard! Klifford!

He was waiting outside the costume room, since I was trying on dresses.

Last night, my father had said some pretty heavy stuff to me, but I'd decided to shut it all deep in my mind and basically not worry about it. You know what they say, poison can become medicine if used correctly!

And Klifford was my Adjutant—if I couldn't depend on him, then who else could I depend on?! I had a desperate need...for a man's opinion!

"Sasha, could you bring Klifford in here?"

"Er?! You mean...Sir Alderton?"

"I haven't undressed yet—shouldn't that be permissible? I wish to ask a man's opinion in the selection of my dress. And Klifford is the perfect choice."

"But, Princess..." Sasha glanced at Matilda.

Matilda nodded at Sasha and checked in with me. "Your Highness... are you certain you are fine with Sir Alderton entering this space?"

"Is there anything wrong with it?" I asked.

The costume room was split in two parts: the room we were

standing in and a changing room where I would climb into the dresses. Since Klifford wouldn't be in the changing room with me, I couldn't see any problem with it…unless the mere act of entering the costume room was an unforgivable offense even for a bodyguard. No boys allowed?

"Oh, no, Your Highness. I am simply relieved to see the high level of trust you've cultivated with your bodyguard. That fact is more than enough justification to allow it."

G-gee, Matilda, laying it on a little thick, aren't we…?

Matilda smiled and nodded. "You have us here to tend to you as well, and above all else, this is your wish. I have no problem with it. Sasha?"

"Yes, ma'am. I shall go fetch him."

Sasha handed Matilda the dress she was holding and stepped out into the hallway where Klifford was waiting.

A minute later, Sasha returned with Klifford. The moment he set foot into the costume room, he gave it a cautious once-over, just like he had done that day he entered my bedchamber. Was it, like, a knight's tic? Scanning for threats? Or scoping out the floor plan?

Lastly, his gaze fell on me. He was probably wondering why I'd asked for him.

"Klifford, there's something I wish to ask of you."

"If there's anything I can do to help, it would be my pleasure."

"Matilda, Sasha, if you'll please."

Matilda and Sasha were standing several feet away from Klifford. Each was holding up their dress in a way that the full silhouette could be seen.

"Sir Alderton, this green dress is a most fashionable color…"

"But Her Highness prefers softer colors, so don't get too wrapped up in the color…"

Matilda and Sasha, seemingly confident in their dresses, each talked up their respective choice's merits. Hierarchy of chief lady-in-waiting and handmaid momentarily put aside, there were sparks flying between them. But throughout the fierce competition, each competently explained to Klifford (in a way he could understand) which dresses were currently popular and which designs I preferred. *Ladies' competition sure is fierce.*

Once I determined they'd both had enough time to state their cases, I spoke up. "I will be attending the junior ball tomorrow. I wish to wear one of these two dresses, but all of us here are ladies. I wish to have a gentleman's opinion."

Klifford stared at the two dresses for quite some time, sizing them up. Then he glanced toward the closet and returned his gaze to me.

I'm trapped in a deep-blue gaze…!

Then eventually, Klifford finally looked away and said, "Your Highness…that fan you carry with you daily, do you intend to carry it at the junior ball as well?"

My fan? It's sitting on the desk right now…

"But of course."

It's a one-of-a-kind item! I take pride in the fact that it will be an accessory that I can bring to the junior ball without shame! If I wave it in front of my face with a smile, everyone will interpret my actions favorably—it's a necessity for social functions! Then again…I have yet to use my fan in the aforementioned social functions. The last time my fan made an appearance was…at the ball last year—though I used a white fan that time.

Klifford nodded in understanding. "I think your chief lady-in-waiting's dress and your handmaid's dress are both quite grand. Either would suit you beautifully, Your Highness."

In spite of his praise, Klifford showed no sign of expressing a preference. "However…with all due respect, Your Highness, may I be permitted to suggest a third dress?"

"Well!"

"Oh my."

I followed Matilda's and Sasha's surprised exclamations with my own, "*You*, Klifford?" My eyelids fluttered in disbelief.

"Yes, Princess."

"Hmm... Very well."

It was an unexpected suggestion, but I *was* interested to see what kind of dress Klifford would choose. You'll never know until you try, right?

12

With a bow, Klifford turned and walked to the closet.

The dresses in the closet were generally sorted by color. Klifford headed straight to the side with primary-colored dresses and grabbed one of them.

"Sir Alderton, hand it to me," Matilda said. She took the dress and walked it over to me so I could get a better look at it.

The midsection of the dress was red, and the rest of it was black. It was a draped design with bright accents of pearl. It was off-the-shoulder in a unique way. It came with a detachable long black cloth that was affixed to the left shoulder—the one that was sleeved.

It used two of the colors Matilda had said were popular, and being off-the-shoulder, it also showed a little skin. Its selling point had to be that detachable bolt of cloth!

But it seemed that Klifford's priorities had been different. "I think this dress will complement your fan, Your Highness."

I took my fan off the desk and opened it, spreading its black feathers wide. And sure enough, the dresses that Matilda and Sasha had proudly chosen—while they were each complete in their own way—their unique designs would probably clash with my fan. My accessory of choice would have stuck out like a sore thumb.

Whereas my everyday dresses were each colored and designed in such a way that they could go with anything...though they weren't particularly chosen with my fan in mind.

I brought my fan close to the dual-colored dress Klifford had chosen. His choice was also quite bold and unique, yet it was a perfect match for my fan.

"So you mean to say you chose that dress to go with my fan?"

"You are well-known as Princess Blackfeather, Your Highness. If you intend on carrying that black fan with you to the junior ball, then it would be best to select a dress that would let your fan shine."

"Princess...Blackfeather?" I furrowed my brow.

Um, Klifford? That nickname you just said...I kinda can't let it slide.

Klifford remained unruffled. "The feathers in your fan are from the wreven bird. Am I wrong, Your Highness?"

Wrevens—the generous source of my fan's materials—were large black birds that you could see flying around anywhere. I even saw them often from within the castle grounds, and sometimes they'd drop a feather.

"You are not wrong, Klifford," I confirmed.

Then he elaborated, "Wrevens are reviled as unlucky birds. Most of the fans carried by ladies of the aristocracy are made of white feathers. However, in making and carrying that fan, you have shattered both of these rules. Now, black fans are in style, and people have even started feeding wrevens. That is why you are known as Princess Blackfeather."

Wh-why did they have to give me such a cringey nickname?! Nooo! Somebody kill meeee! Oh, but this sweet, fluffy feeling—you can only get it from wreven feathers!

"You are, however, the only person who uses a fan made of wreven feathers, Your Highness. At least, as far as I've seen."

Wh-why, though?

Hearing it put that way, I suddenly felt like stanning wrevens. Like, why are they unlucky? What did they ever do to you? Don't get me wrong, it's not like I want everyone to pluck out wreven feathers when they aren't even molting and make a buttload of fans—I just want everyone to know how great they are! I must explain their wonders!

"I'll have you know, wreven feathers are superb. Anyone would agree they are grand if they would just use them."

He answered innocently, "Perhaps they're afraid."

"Afraid?"

Of birds?

"It is said that wrevens are an omen of death. The followers of Saza believe in aerial familiars used by the Goddess of Death who rules over Hell. Wrevens' bad reputation began when they were said to resemble these birds."

The Saza faith's...Hell...

"By Hell...do you mean Ongarne?"

Hearing the word *Hell* made the events of the Turchen Arc pop into my mind. The name of *Ongarne* originated from the Saza followers, I think.

Klifford's lips turned into a slight smile. I think he was...enjoying himself?

"Yes, Your Highness. They are birds from Ongarne, the deepest layer of Hell. One might even say that wrevens are familiars of Ongarne itself."

In other words, ordinary black feathers were welcome in high fashion, but wreven feathers were a no-no. I guess it was like wearing all black anywhere outside a funeral? Or like walking around with a bunch of occult items?

That explains it! That's why when I brought in the feathers and babbled excitedly about what I wanted, the fan maker frowned so hard at me... So the color...and the bird...are both cringe?

C'mon, fan maker! Ya could've at least told me! Wait, unless it was common knowledge that I should already have known? How stupid! I mean, it never came up in my royal studies! How did everybody else find out about it?

But it's too late... I'm already obsessed with this fan. The large, fluffy feathers alone are enough to make wrevens the best birds in my book! Besides, the whole "Ongarne's familiar" thingy is mere superstition! I mean, I'm still alive, aren't I? Yup!

"Your Highness," Matilda said, taking a step forward. "About Blackfeather... I implore you to reconsider it."

Aha. So even Matilda, my chief lady-in-waiting, has taken to calling my fan Blackfeather!

"Everyone here at the castle is used to seeing you with Blackfeather. And if it were merely a fan that happened to be black, no one would think it strange that you would use it—social standing aside. But, Your Highness, your Blackfeather is fashioned from wreven feathers. This will be your first junior ball in a while, and people might gossip about you. So perhaps you should consider leaving Blackfeather at home just this once?"

She was only making that suggestion because she was worried about me.

"Thank you, Matilda."

I'll thank you...for now.

But you see... This fan has practically become an extension of my body! Without its soothing fluffiness, I cannot possibly escape that hellhole of a junior ball alive!

And if carrying this fan makes people call me Princess Blackfeather... then instead of ditching my fan, I'll double down and adopt the cringey nickname willingly!

"Yes, but I am Princess Blackfeather, no? Perhaps I was invited in hopes that I *would* bring Blackfeather with me."

"Forgive me... I mean no disrespect, Your Highness. But I can't shake the worry that Blackfeather might draw death your way..."

I guess Matilda's the superstitious type? I had no idea. In practice, I highly doubt that carrying a fan made of wreven feathers would lead to an untimely death...but I guess it's a matter of the heart. I need to do something to reassure Matilda...

"A bodyguard is assigned to royals so that such a thing won't happen, no?"

"A bodyguard... You mean Sir Alderton?"

"Why, yes. I do." I smiled at Matilda, then looked up at Klifford. His indigo eyes stared back at mine. "Klifford. If I carry Blackfeather with me, you will protect me from any theoretical death, yes?"

Come on, Klifford, this is where you answer quickly, even if you don't mean it! Please, do it for Matilda!

"Yes, Princess. I feel that it is *because* you carry Blackfeather that I am most suited to protect you."

Ooh. Looks like Klifford kinda really likes this fan. My kindred spirit!

I forgot I was a princess and grinned up at Klifford. *You get it! You recognize the splendor of wreven feathers!*

"And I appreciate your loyalty," I answered. "Well, if you feel that strongly about it, Klifford...then perhaps I should give you a wreven feather of your own?"

For a spur of the moment idea, that was pretty ingenious if I do say so myself! I still hadn't given Klifford a gift from our oath ritual, after all. Then again, the whole thing turned into a Sovereign and Adjutant ritual...

But I think a Sovereign giving her Adjutant a gift could be a thing. And since men can't exactly carry fans...I think he could use a feather in some other way.

"You wish to give me a wreven feather..."

Klifford's lips turned upward at the ends. It looked like he was trying not to laugh.

"If I am Princess Blackfeather, then as my bodyguard, you should also carry a wreven feather, no? It is a most reasonable suggestion."

Besides, you're a wreven feather lover like me! We're birds of a feather, you and I!

"Might I suggest a feathered tassel for your sword?"

The tip of his sword hilt currently had a tassel on it. It wasn't something you'd see on the average soldier's sword. But knights or soldiers above a certain rank would have one. It was a status symbol.

But wouldn't it get in the way when you fought, you may ask...if you're a normie! It was more than mere decoration. In an expert's hand, this tassel could be used to feint an attack...or so I've heard.

Klifford's tassel appeared to be the castle's standard-issue. Among the nobility, that little tassel served as a major form of self-expression. They came in a variety of materials, colors, and lengths. It was surprising that Klifford's tassel was standard-issue, given that House Alderton was famous for its military prowess...but perhaps Klifford just wasn't that interested in them.

"However, I won't force it on you. This is nothing more than a whim of mine."

When I love something, I wanna spread it far and wide! I want everyone in the world to love it, too! But you can't force it. Ever!

In my past life...I failed big-time when I tried to get a friend of mine who liked to read shoujo novels to give *The Noble King* a try. She kept evasively avoiding my recommendation. But I wanted her to read it so badly that I got even more determined and pushed it on her relentlessly. Until one day, my friend said to me, *"I don't care how good it is—I just don't like BL stuff!"*

I know, I was wrong... So I apologized to her, and we patched things up.

Before her, I knew plenty of girls who didn't think they'd be crazy about BL, but they at least gave it a try without much resistance...and wound up becoming major *fujoshi*. That's why my senses had dulled completely.

No matter how much you love something, there are going to be people who just don't like it. You must remember to *never* force your special interest onto someone! No matter how much you love it...you must promote it with a measured hand.

You've gotta respect people's free will!

Hoo-boy, that was a close call. In my ardent advocacy of wreven feathers, I very nearly got carried away! Okay, Octavia, let's dial it back a few notches!

"If you dislike the idea, feel free to say no. I wouldn't fault you for it," I said, waiting for his reply.

"If it is a gift from you, Your Highness...then I gladly accept it."

Maybe it was his lingering stifled laugh...but unless my eyes deceived me, he looked devilish.

"I look forward to it. And when I receive the tassel of wreven feathers..." He gestured at his sword. "Then I will affix it here."

Not only was he going to accept the gift—he was actually going to use it. That definitely made Klifford and I birds of a wreven feather!

All riiight! I'd better put in an order with the artisan who made my fan!

Someone giggled. It was Matilda.

"It would seem I worried for nothing," she said, smiling warmly at us. "As long as you have Sir Alderton in your service, Your Highness, then you will be just fine."

Then she bowed. "Forgive me for speaking out of turn."

"Oh, no. I am grateful to you, Matilda."

"Let me ask just to make sure, Your Highness. Which dress are you choosing?"

The dark green dress, the pale blue dress, and the red-and-black dress. As long as this fan of mine was a mandatory item...

"I'll go with the dress Klifford selected."

As single items, the other two dresses were just as good. But to match Blackfeather...I had to go with dress number three.

I have spoken.

"It surprises me how good you are at choosing dresses, Sir Alderton. Though it vexes me a little to say so... I was really proud of my selection," Sasha said as she looked down at the pale blue dress in her arms.

"Well, aside from Count Alderton and Sir Alderton here, House Alderton is all ladies," Matilda said. "Perhaps they cultivated such an understanding in you?"

Klifford shook his head. "I have three sisters—one elder and two younger than I. Unfortunately...they dislike me. They never asked me to help choose their dresses, and even if they did, I am uncertain whether or not I could live up to their expectations."

"Oh, and why is that?" I asked quizzically. It seemed like the sort of task Klifford could easily carry out.

"The only reason I was able to choose a dress for you, Your Highness, was because of Blackfeather."

"Because I always carry it with me?"

"That is part of the reason, yes, but... In a way, Blackfeather is your weapon, Your Highness. So I was able to think of your dress in the same way that I think of my uniform on the battlefield. One first chooses a weapon, then one chooses one's uniform to accompany the weapon."

So he applied the same principle to dress selection...

"Your weapon *is* your life?"

"Aye."

"Meaning my greatest weapon of all is not my dress but my fan, I suppose."

"Did I offend you, Your Highness?"

"Heavens no. In fact, you've made me quite happy to have a dress for the junior ball. Thank you, Klifford."

I opened my fan in front of my face and smiled sweetly at him.

All that remained was to try on the dress and have it fitted. Then there were the rest of my accessories and my shoes to decide on!

13

I moved into the changing room. There was a mirror inside, and it was a space wide enough to fit about ten people. All my handmaids aside from Sasha were with me, and it was time to begin the fitting. I stood before the giant mirror, obeying my handmaids' instructions to raise my arms, lower my arms...or suck in my tummy. Luckily, my dress didn't need to be altered much.

My handmaids stepped back. That was the signal for *Please move on your own and see how it fits.*

I looked in the mirror and did a twirl. The cloth on my shoulder fluttered behind me. The gather in the skirt was not overdone—it was just right. It was easy to move in. And now that I had it on, I could see it didn't expose my skin as much as I thought it would.

Yup! I think it passes. I'll toot my own horn.

"Here you go, Your Highness," Sasha said, handing me my fan.

"Thank you." I took the unfortunately named Blackfeather in my hand. I opened it with a flourish and held it in front of my chest.

I'd say that my face—Octavia's face, rather—was of the cute, girlish variety. My overall image, from my hair to my eyes, was very muted. Pale...like a ghost? Charitably put, I looked soft and gentle. Uncharitably put, I was lacking in royal dignity. It was like, no matter how tall I stood, I couldn't ditch my milksop appearance. Even if I somehow corrected the sense of self I still had engraved in my consciousness from my past life—no matter how much like a princess I talked or moved, I still looked like a smug little brat. And I think it's all because of my features!

But all that has changed now...because of this dress and fan. Synergetic effect, you might call it? I looked in the mirror, and a princess smiled back at me. I looked much more noble than usual!

"My goodness...I feel like we've produced a whole new side to you, Your Highness. What do you say? Should we order a few more dresses similar to this for your daily wear?"

I had more than enough everyday dresses already. But it was a very tempting offer. I figured maybe I should take the opportunity.

"That sounds like a good idea, Sasha."

As I said this, I caught a glimpse in the corner of the mirror of Matilda walking into the changing room. She had been absent during the fitting process.

"You look lovely in that dress, Your Highness."

"Thank you, Matilda."

"I've brought the accessories you requested."

Matilda was carrying a tray of jewelry. She nodded to a handmaid, who entered after her with a pair of shoes and placed them before my feet.

There was a pendant of large sapphires on Matilda's tray. And the shoes were silver with delicate embroidery. Most notable were the shoe's heels, which were comfortably short.

As I stood before the mirror and watched myself try on each new item, I pondered what jewelry and shoes to wear. The dress was my biggest hurdle, so now I was free to choose the rest of my outfit on my own.

Besides, most of my accessories were royal heirlooms or pieces with an eye-popping number of gemstones, so they were strictly supervised. It's not like we could all gather 'round and harmoniously choose something together. The only person who could access their storage space besides the royal family was my chief lady-in-waiting, Matilda.

And as for the shoes, well, I chose them not for their design but for how comfy they were to walk in! There's no way anyone besides me could choose them. Wearing a brand-new pair to the junior ball would just be way too painful. Especially for my feet!

As I slowly stared at my dressed-up reflection in the mirror, I deliberated carefully. Then I asked Matilda to bring me two accessories.

For my jewelry, since I hated wearing anything jingly but knew that wearing no jewelry would be a terrible faux pas, I chose a pendant. It had a large, oblong-cut sapphire in the center. Its color was slightly purple. It was worn by princesses in generations past, so it was both traditional and formal.

For my shoes, I chose a pair that were designed for formal occasions, but I'd also worn them a few times, so they were already broken in. Most royalty and noblewomen wore high-heeled shoes. They made you stand taller and made your legs look longer, after all.

However…they were not made for walking long distances. And castles were big. And my primary method of transport was walking. And what does walking all day in high-heeled shoes do to your feet, you may ask? It ruins your feet, that's what! It makes you dependent on pre-bedtime foot massages! And do I subject my poor handmaids to that work, you may ask? Well, no. I go with low-heeled shoes.

With high-class ladies' shoes, appearance is everything. But for women on the move, comfort is everything. So I introduced the latter into the selection. And these silver shoes struck just the right balance.

I put on these two final articles and retouched my makeup a little. I had a handmaid tie up part of my hair, and then I was done.

Lastly, I took my shoes for a spin and walked around in the changing room. It didn't feel like I'd get any blisters, so I was good to go for the junior ball! Higher-heeled shoes demanded too much dance skill from their wearer. But with these shoes, even if I danced or was on my feet for a long time, my feet wouldn't hurt then, nor would they hurt the next day...

Wait...dance?

My brows furrowed.

"Your Highness, why don't we show Sir Alderton how you look?" Sasha asked.

"We think that would be a good idea," Matilda added with a nod.

"Yes, of course...," I answered, hiding my sudden restlessness.

D-A-N-C-E! I'd completely forgotten! A junior ball always came with dancing!

Oh, of course I'd learned how to dance. It was drilled into me from an early age. But back then, since an adult partner would be way too big a height difference, my big brother insisted on being my dance partner. He was great at taking the lead. Whenever I'd almost step on his toes, he'd always gracefully sidestep me. What's more, his high-level dancing helped correct my dance steps.

He made dancing so easy for me that I got kinda full of myself and was like, *Whoa, am I, like, a good dancer?* It looked so difficult, but once I gave it a try, it was a piece of cake!

I'd also mastered my dancing lessons...so I started ditching them. Oh, what a terrifying monster I used to be!

Of course, my cockiness had come back to bite me in the ass.

Tragedy struck when I was ten years old. While I had been seen here and there before, that was supposed to be my first formal appearance as princess of the royal family...at my first royal ball.

That's when The Incident happened. First, I danced with Sirius. That went well. No problems there. My big brother covered for my crappy dancing like a champ.

But when it was time to dance with my next partner...I screwed up.

A merchant's son asked me for a dance. At the time, he was a rising star among merchants. And since my father's partner, Edgar, was a former merchant, we used to let a lot of merchants into the castle grounds.

I happily accepted his request for a dance. I mean, even if he only asked me to dance because his father told him to, this was still a boy my age asking me for a dance, you know?

After watching all the boys dancing intimately with each other—and standing there, enviously twiddling my thumbs—there was no reason for little me to turn him down.

I imagined myself dancing in perfect sync with him... That's how I wished it had gone down.

But our dance ended in misery. In *tears*. I sucked so bad at dancing. Meanwhile, my partner's dance ability was probably average. But I kept stepping on his feet so much that the question *Is that supposed to be dancing?* brought the evening to an awkward end.

I was supposed to dance more, but I was so overwhelmed that I retreated into my shell. Filled with regret, I sent a letter to the merchant's son that simply said: *I'm sorry...* But he didn't answer. Right after I'd sent the letter, the merchant was arrested for selling sketchy goods in an illegitimate market or something like that.

Maybe that was the reason why merchant attendance was drastically reduced at the next ball...

So those're the tragic details of my first dance.

The very next day, I threw myself into my dance lessons. I tried. I really did try. Until eventually, I went from sucky...to average! But my dance trauma still runs deep.

I'll dance when I'm asked for one, and I'm at least at a point now where my dancing isn't painfully awkward to watch. But I do still have a major gap in my experience from avoiding junior balls like the plague all those years.

I barely attended royal balls as it is...but in all the royal balls, I only danced with family!

The last person I danced with was Alec, at last year's royal ball. And just like Sirius, Alec possesses that special power to skillfully bring up my average dancing to a pro level! My baby brother is too amazing for his own good! So it didn't matter if I danced well with Alec—it was all because of Alec!

"Come, Your Highness," Sasha urged.

"All right…"

Sasha escorted me from the changing room to the costume room. I looked at the floor the whole time, my head filled with dance anxiety.

Come on, Octavia, get a hold of yourself! Just rely on your muscle memory, and you should be okay. I just need to practice dancing before Countess Reddington's junior ball…

"Sir Alderton, what do you think of Her Highness's outfit?" Matilda asked Klifford.

Klifford?

I looked up. His indigo eyes met mine. He had probably waited in the costume room all that time. Maybe Matilda had told him to.

It's a nice gesture and all…

But before Klifford could say anything, I spoke first. "Klifford, can you dance?" I was sure I had a ghastly look in my eyes.

"I have…some knowledge of it?"

He passes!

"I simply must practice my dancing. Be my partner."

Your princess orders you! You cannot refuse!

As I was already wearing my planned ensemble for the junior ball, this would be a perfect simulation. What's more, I doubted Klifford had the dance prowess of either of my brothers. As Count Alderton's adoptive son, he probably only had rudimentary dance lessons.

If I could pull off a dance with Klifford without messing up too badly, that would prove my dancing hadn't regressed!

With just Sasha and Matilda as our audience, Klifford and I faced each other in the center of the practice room. We had to make do with a practice room, since the great hall that was used for royal balls was out of the question. This room was also soundproof.

As I stood in that room, I was haunted by the ghosts of those desperate days I was forced to practice my dancing here...

Ordinarily, one needed a live musician to be present in order to practice dancing...but this was a castle. We had a secret weapon no one else had. A *pianola*—a self-playing piano! It came with an extensive collection of dance repertoire, too!

"But I am your bodyguard, Your Highness..."

"In dancing, weapons are not necessary. In the dance hall, I give Blackfeather to someone else for safekeeping."

Klifford finally set his sword aside, showing discomfort all the while. As my bodyguard, protecting me was his job. Setting his sword aside was an outrageous notion. But he couldn't dance with a sword at his belt, either.

The practice room held only the four of us: Klifford, Sasha, Matilda, and myself. We kept the party as small as possible in the name of security. That way, as long as Matilda and Sasha weren't spies, there was very little chance I would be in danger.

"If anything, as a man with a sword, you are the biggest danger in this room, no?"

It wasn't until I said this that Klifford finally seemed to agree with me.

"You are absolutely correct, Your Highness... I shall set it aside, then."

He gave me a good looking over, then he handed his sword to Matilda with a sigh.

Without his sword—temporary though it was—Klifford seemed much less comfortable than usual. What a refreshing sight it was. It was *because* he normally didn't show much emotion that it was easy to see the difference.

"Does the absence of your sword worry you?"

"I spend very little time without my sword."

"But I never said you had to remove all your other weapons, did I?"

I knew that as someone whose livelihood was fighting, Klifford was bound to have a few smaller weapons tucked away here and there. At the very least, he must have had one. Everybody was different, though. Gray, my former bodyguard and first love, had explained it all to me.

As a result, I got really into playing the game Spot the Weapon. You look at knights and soldiers and try to guess where they keep their hidden weapons. Aw, memories... If only Gray could see me now. Too bad he quit and left right after he broke my heart...

Spot the Weapon, eh?

I looked Klifford up and down, focusing on his clothing and armor. He wore the indigo uniform reserved only for bodyguards. It was adorned with the royal crest, which was flower-shaped and added an air of beauty and importance to whoever wore it. If it didn't suit you, you looked unbearably bad in it. Only hotties could pull off that look... Oh, that uniform was a cruel mistress!

But anyway, I had no idea where Klifford was hiding his spare weapons. There was nothing amiss about him. The guy was impeccable!

"That reminds me...I heard you were good at playing Spot the Weapon."

"Oh, you know that game, Klifford? I played it during my childhood."

"Yes. Your chief lady-in-waiting told me about it."

"Matilda. You sly vixen..."

I hope she didn't tell him other embarrassing stories about me.

"She told me that you discovered a spy by playing Spot the Weapon."

"A spy..."

Yep, I sure did! That actually happened. After all, it was linked to the tale of my first love. And it caused quite the ruckus in the castle.

"Well, that weapon was too obvious."

"Oh really now?"

Well, yeah, obvious for a girl who was in love with Gray and wanted to impress him so she played Spot the Weapon almost constantly! After enough practice, you're bound to start noticing a few common hiding places. So anyone who deviated from the basic locations was painfully easy to spot. It was all uniform—maybe because soldiers were all given orders from their superiors on where to hide their spare weapons. Some locations were just a pretty safe bet, I guess.

"Well, he was hiding his spare in an unusual place. Besides, he didn't like that I was playing Spot the Weapon."

I was a princess and a little girl. Everyone in the castle always humored me in my little game of Spot the Weapon. So anyone who didn't want to play was *extremely* suspicious. What's more, the guy kept trying to talk to me.

I was scared and ran to Gray for help...and I just happened to be right. Gray was dreadfully handsome as his sword clashed with the spy's—I fell in love with him all over again. Too bad Gray fell in love with another guy and left me right after that.

Oh, incidentally, the spy was after Alec. That's why he kept trying to talk to me. His master had ordered him to kidnap Alec. Apparently, the fifty-year-old geezer had the hots for Alec, who was only ten years old at the time... *Sigh.* Anyway...

I mean, Alec is and always has been an angel, you know? So I can sympathize with the old guy... Like hell! The fact that it saved Alec more than proves that my little game was nothing to sneeze at. Yup.

"I see. Well, would you like to play Spot the Weapon with me?" Klifford asked.

I shook my head. "I already tried. And I lost. I don't think my Spot the Weapon tactics work on you."

Klifford's mouth twitched. "You mean to say...I am also unusual?"

I had to admit, Klifford was cut differently from the rest of my bodyguards thus far. His origin of birth was part of it, but also, the fact that he hadn't fallen in love with another guy yet! But if I agreed with Klifford and acknowledged he was "unusual," that would basically be the same as me saying I think he's a spy.

Hmm... What should I say?

"But you don't object to the game of Spot the Weapon, no? You may be unusual compared to the others here...but what's most important is what happens next. You see, the intruder protested, but...what would you say if I asked you to tell me where you keep your secret weapons?"

A spy would never reveal his secret, you see! Besides, I'm kinda really curious to find out where Klifford keeps his special sword hidden.

"I wouldn't mind it at all."

Good! Correct answer.

"I only hope that you are not disillusioned by what you see, Your Highness..."

I guess I was jumping the gun when I assumed he wouldn't tell me.

"I hide daggers in my sleeve and in my shoe. I assume these are rather ordinary hiding places."

"Oh...why, yes, they are."

"Did you find my answer rather boring, Your Highness?"

Not boring, exactly...but they were rather ordinary hiding places. I hadn't expected that. But even a quick body scan showed no daggers whatsoever. It gave me pause.

But just think, he's still worried without his longsword, even with two spare daggers? What a burden... Occupational hazard, much?

The music began to play. Everything was ready for us. The pianola was playing a dancing tune titled *Hofballtanze* by the composer Weisen. He lived a long life during King Eus's reign and composed many dance pieces.

Hofballtanze was a classic of the classics. It was really catchy and popular, too, so it was bound to be played at the junior ball.

"Princess Octavia...may I have this dance?"

I followed procedure and answered him politely, "Yes, thank you." I followed with a soft nod.

"Your hand, please."

He extended the palm of his hand to me, and I rested my right hand on it. He squeezed my hand and tugged me close to him. And his free hand slid around the small of my back.

14

My muscles still remembered the dance steps. I could move just fine to the rhythm of the music. And as for Klifford...well, he wasn't as skilled as my brothers, but he was definitely above average. For someone who hastily learned how to dance after being adopted by House Alderton, he was more than good. Was he just physically gifted? He seemed very secure.

Except...he didn't seem entirely loyal to the fundamentals. At times, his own style would butt in. Like, he would half-ass the most difficult steps in time with the music.

It wasn't a competition—we weren't going to be scored or anything. And even though he needed to only look the part, he did have some nerve dancing that way. Still, thanks to Klifford, my tight nerves started to unwind. I decided not to strive for a dance with no mistakes but to be able to recover from mistakes when I made them.

The most important part of dancing is that you have fun!

And in just a few minutes, my confidence grew. *Good. I'm not stepping on Klifford's toes, and I haven't made any major mistakes. Progress! I've got this! I should be able to dance just fine at the junior ball now!*

Without even looking in the mirror, I knew there was a big smile of relief filling my face. Then I saw Klifford, my dancing partner, smirk a little. It wasn't that lip-twitch sort of a half smile I'd seen countless times from him, but a softer smile. And...it was kind of incredibly lethal, you know! This's why I hated super-fine specimens!

"......"
"......"

An uncomfortably long silence hung between us...and the relief I'd gained from dancing was overshadowed by an entirely new problem. When I'd had all my concentration set on dancing okay, I hadn't thought much of it, but... *Klifford...isn't he a little too close to me? This proximity is bad for my heart.*

Besides, Klifford was so outstanding that I wouldn't have been surprised if he'd fallen in love with someone else and quit being my guard a long time ago. That's just how hot he was.

And you mean to tell me I was dancing just fine with this hottie for several minutes?!

Of course, it's only natural when I'm dancing with a partner! But I don't feel the calmness I felt dancing with Alec... Why am I so anxious?!

When you danced with a partner, you had to look him in the eye as much as possible. That's what I was taught, and I was doing just fine with it up until that point. But when he looked back at me, I casually looked away.

"Your Highness?"

Klifford's handsome voice struck me right in the heart.

Yeah, I guess looking away from him the whole time we're dancing is gonna seem rude... Come on, look back at Klifford. Urgh! God dammit, he's so hot! My cheeks are burning—I've gotta stop them from turning red!

T-talk! Yes, a conversation! That'll help distract me!

God...the Hofballtanze *is so frickin' long... It's a full ten minutes. Judging by where we're at in the melody, we're probably at the three-minute mark... Oh, wait... This is the part where there's a bunch of tricky steps! You need to brace yourself, Octavia! Yeah, yeah, I know.*

At an actual dance, you'd change partners. Of course, if you wanted to stay with your partner, that was also an option. But...Klifford was the only other dancer here.

And to make matters worse... *Um, Klifford? Excuse me, but why have your eyes been glued to me all this time?*

I felt like I was in a trance—as if not a single movement of mine would escape his gaze.

Is there something on my face? There isn't, right?

Urgh!

Th-that's what you get for overthinking this, Octavia! All your experiences so far have taught you that there's a one hundred percent chance your bodyguard will run off with some other guy! And Klifford may have

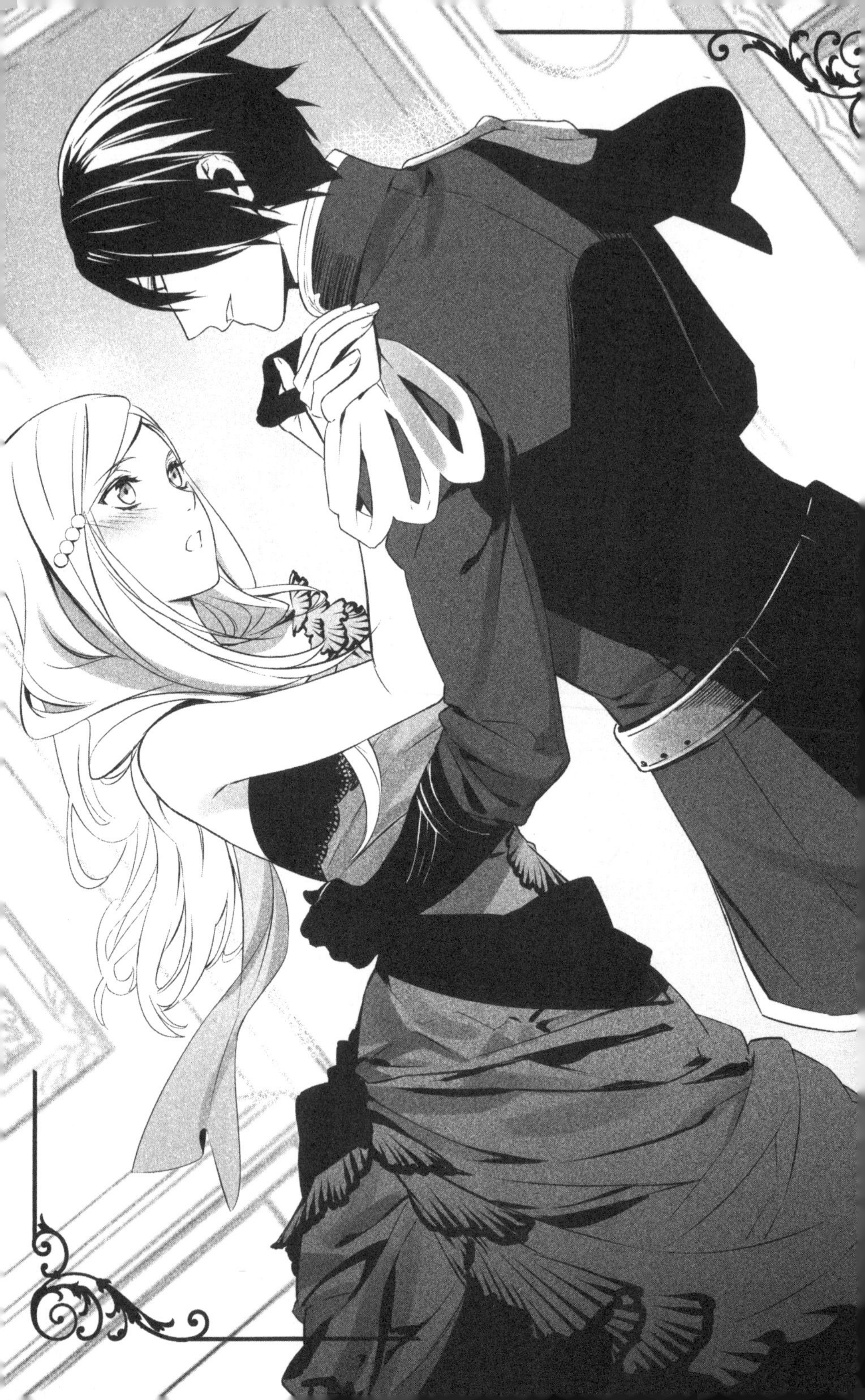

promised to serve you, but that doesn't guarantee that he won't hook up with some guy.

You can't perceive him as a man. You can't let yourself swoon. Bodyguards are out of the question. Out of the question... I know you want to fall in love, but there's nothing dumber than falling in love with a guy who's absolutely gonna break your heart!

"S-so your hidden weapons are daggers... Are blades your specialty, then?"

We were talking about weapons right up until we started dancing, so I might as well resume that convo to get my mind off things! I shall murder what makes my heart float on air! Be still, my swooning heart!

Klifford stared at me blankly. Then he looked down. He actually seemed stumped by the question. It was a relief to have his gaze off me. It's a good thing he was my ally—if somebody told me that Klifford's death glare could shorten my life span, I'd believe them.

"Generally, I am comfortable with blades, yes..."

I see, I see. He's the jack-of-all-trades type.

"I suppose I am most skilled with the sword. But the weapon I feel most comfortable using would be a spear."

"A spear..."

I twirled a full rotation. My skirt billowed out with me. Then I returned to Klifford's arms. This was the part of the music where the tempo slowed down and there was a short break in the dancing.

"Yes. I can thrust, stab, and throw a spear. Unlike a sword, I need not be near my enemy to defeat him, so spears are very useful in battle. They're also quite effective when you need to swing them around. However...a spear is not suitable for my everyday equipment. Neither is one suitable to protect you, Your Highness."

"Well, yes. That does make sense."

Where would you even carry a spear? On your back? It's much longer than a sword, so yeah, it would get in the way if you wore one indoors.

"But in battle, I would ideally carry both a sword and a spear. This is my personal preference, of course."

He does seem like a war veteran...so I guess he has fought on the battlefield. And that's what made him catch Count Alderton's eye. Is that also how my father learned about him?

As I wandered, lost in thought, the dance steps brought our bodies close together.

"Is something the matter, Your Highness?"

He was so close that I could feel his breath on my lips. So close that nobody could hear us speak. His deep indigo eyes were like vortexes… I could see my reflection in them. Did that mean Klifford could see himself in my eyes, too? I felt my heart—which I thought had finally calmed down—beat a little faster again.

"I was thinking about you, Klifford."

"About…me?"

"My father…His Majesty is wary of you, and I was wondering why. Aside from last night…you've spoken with him before, haven't you?"

This time, I was the one who wouldn't let a single one of his movements escape my gaze. But Klifford, not particularly fazed by it, gazed right back at me.

"When I was appointed as your bodyguard…His Majesty did approach me. He appeared to be very worried about you, Your Highness."

"Father was…worried?"

"Perhaps it was because you chose someone like me to be your bodyguard? His Majesty loves you deeply, Your Highness."

Just a hunch…but I probably had a very doubtful look in my eyes right then. *Father…loves me? I know we're family, but not only is he not my real father by blood, but we hardly ever talk—how could he possibly love me? I'm not too sure I fully believe that.*

"You needn't protect my feelings, Klifford," I said, shaking my head. *Surely, my father neither likes nor dislikes me. There was no way he'd worry about me as a daughter, let alone love me.*

Klifford's eyes widened a little. "You think…I'm protecting your feelings?"

Then he chuckled. His voice shook deeply with laughter.

The pause in the dancing was over. We had now reached the climax of the *Hofballtanze*, where both partners required skill to execute the tricky dance steps.

Since we had the entire practice room to ourselves, we could move about however we wished. If we danced it well…it could be a lot of fun!

We spun around together as we danced.

"Was it really necessary for you to laugh?"

"Forgive me, Your Highness. It's just, lying to protect someone's feelings is a concept so foreign to me…"

"You mean to say tact doesn't suit you?"

"At the very least, I would doubt my ears if someone who knows what I am said that about me." Klifford smirked. His eyes shone like a wild beast's.

"Someone who knows…that you are an Adjutant?"

"Yes. As well as those who—in becoming residents of Ongarne—discovered that I am an Adjutant… Your Highness, an Adjutant cannot tell a lie to his Sovereign."

His words cut me like a knife. "Forgive me…I was wrong."

I sighed. I had decided not to let my father's words get to me…but that "poison" line really did seem to have left a deep mark on me. Even though he had told me that I was the only living person who knew he was an Adjutant, I'd asked him a question that showed I didn't trust him.

"I wasn't taking myself seriously as your Sovereign… Tell me, Klifford, what sort of Sovereign would you like me to be?"

Adjutant and Sovereign—Klifford and I—if you compared the two of us, I personally think the Adjutant's stats were way overpowered! I needed to become the ideal Sovereign so that Klifford wouldn't be frustrated by me.

"Well…would you please give me a command as my Sovereign?"

A command?

I'd asked him what he wished of me, but he threw a curveball right back at me.

When a few seconds had passed without my answering him,

Klifford's eyes shadowed over. "Won't you give a command to your Adjutant, Your Highness?"

When I noticed his gaze lacked its usual sharp gleam, my little fangirl heart threatened to go back into swoon mode.

Hey, what's with those puppy dog eyes? How can someone so stoic and cool be so vulnerable? Is this that phenomenon I'd heard of only in name in my past life...the "gap moe" trope? Yikes, that was a close call!

I immediately pumped the brakes on my runaway heart. "Do you mean to say you wish that I give you a special command as your Sovereign?"

"No, Your Highness. However, it brings an Adjutant great joy to grant the wish of his Sovereign. So I would appreciate a command, if possible."

So that's all it is! But it's hard to come up with a command out of nowhere... Hmm, what's a Sovereign-like command...? Oh! I think I've got one.

"If...," I began, an idea popping into my head. "If I ever cry...then I want you to hide me so that nobody can see my tears."

The grip in our clasped hands intensified.

After all, it was possible that in the near future, I'd be crying bitter tears... Nope, it was certain! Either over Sirius or over my botched search for a boyfriend, I could just see myself wailing into a handkerchief!

And the person most likely to witness it happening was the one who's always by my side—my bodyguard, Klifford! He was the perfect cover. *So when the worst happens to your Sovereign, Adjutant...cover my ass, if you please!*

I'm the type of girl who needs to shut herself in her room and cry her eyes out, FYI! I'm also the type of girl who doesn't want anyone to see me at my weakest! But the waterworks don't always wait until I'm alone in my room to come on. And there are times when, try as I might to hold my tears back, I simply can't. Not crying would be my first choice, but you can't always have that.

Klifford remained silent.

"Klifford?"

The climax of the dance would be over soon. Our free hands reached out to each other…then parted.

Klifford's hand then took mine, pulling me back to him, and he whispered, "You do betray one's expectations, Your Highness."

Huh? Nobody's easier to read than me. I live with my heart on my sleeve. Sure, in my life as a princess, I've mastered a few mind games, but mostly, I try to be a straight shooter!

"Are you saying that you want me to force unreasonable demands on you as my Adjutant?"

If so, then I'm disappointed in you, Klifford! When I do use my princess privilege, I always push it to the max…but it only happens sometimes, okay? I don't just pick on my vassals for no reason, you know!

"That's not what I meant. It's just, for a command from a Sovereign to an Adjutant…yours was rather adorable."

"What do you mean?"

Then it hit me. *Wait, was this just a Sovereign test? Like, he'd ask me to give him a command just to see what kind of command I'd give him? Was that smoldering gaze—the one that I accidentally swooned over—just an ingenious ploy to fluster me?*

"Klifford…why did you wish for me to give you a command?"

"A Sovereign giving her Adjutant commands *is* the fastest way for an Adjutant and Sovereign to understand each other. I saw that it was necessary for us, Your Highness. A command weighs heavier than a hundred thousand words."

Called it! It was a Sovereign test!

"I see… So did you come to understand me better?" I asked coolly, my heart nearly exploding inside.

"As I told you earlier, I understood that you are a Sovereign who betrays my expectations. And I have taken your command to heart."

So the command itself took effect, then? I passed the Sovereign test?

"So you'll promise me? That if I should cry…"

Klifford chuckled. "A promise is not necessary. My Sovereign, I shall hide you, if that is your command."

"It is my command." I nodded.

But...the next time he asks me to give him a command as his Sovereign, I'd better tread more carefully. It seems like a command from a Sovereign to an Adjutant carries a lot more weight than I originally thought.

Also...an Adjutant can't lie to his Sovereign, eh? *That's a new revelation.*

When Klifford told me that my father loves me...he wasn't saying that to protect my feelings. He really believed it. Whether it's actually true or not is another matter entirely, but at the very least, he must have had cause for believing it. Unless Klifford's views on love are different from mine?

I turned to ask him about it, but then I noticed Klifford's eyes were directed outside of the practice room—at the hallway. Klifford stopped dancing. I stopped in turn.

"Klifford?"

But the *Hofballtanze* was still playing.

"Your Highness. Behind me."

Klifford whisked me behind him protectively. His hand hovered over the dagger concealed up his sleeve—he could draw it at a moment's notice.

And then the door to the practice room burst open.

"Excuse meee!" a young man called out. He was short of breath—he'd probably run here. But from where I was standing, all I could see was Klifford's back, so I didn't know what the man looked like.

"I come bearing a message from Prince Alexis! I heard that Princess Octavia was here, so I—eep?! Oh!"

Eep? Oh?

As far as I knew, there was no reason to scream inside a practice room. Klifford kept his dagger concealed and stepped to the side. *No problem. Guess that means we're safe?*

Although...Klifford shouldn't have been able to hear a single footstep from that man. But he still sensed that someone was coming and guarded me just in case.

I looked at the practice room intruder. And as you'd guess, I didn't recognize his—*no, wait, huh? I do recognize his face.*

It was the soldier who had been sparring with Alec in the training grounds and left to talk to his colleague.

And when the soldier saw Klifford, all the color drained from his face.

15

A mere soldier delivering a message to a princess...was something that never happened. Communications with me usually went through my handmaids. Whenever I wanted to meet with someone in the castle or deliver a message, I would always summon my handmaid first. And it was true the other way around as well. If somebody wanted to reach me, my handmaid would always approach me first with *"An invitation from Lord So-And-So."*

The only exceptions were soldiers who served as runners. Sometimes, they would come to me directly, depending on the nature of the message. And the runner was a fixed assignment. He was in his forties and had been doing the job for many years. It was a safety measure to ensure that I wouldn't be fooled if, heaven forbid, a fake runner came to me. I mean, whenever a runner came to me, he generally didn't have very good news, so the best runners were the absent ones.

I looked at the soldier before me. His face was still ghostly white. I marveled over how such tanned, healthy-looking skin could still be so visibly drained of color.

Is it because of Klifford? Soldier-boy did go "Eep!" when he saw him. But wait...Klifford's just standing there, isn't he? Even earlier, when it looked like he was going to draw his dagger, he didn't. There was no cause for an Eep! *anywhere.*

Besides, this soldier is young...so he can't be a runner. Hmm... But judging by Klifford's reaction, he determined that this soldier isn't a threat.

And if memory served me correctly, that soldier was acquainted with

Alec. Meaning he was still a little suspicious, but it was quite feasible that he did come with a message from Alec.

But wait, why did Alec send a common foot soldier to deliver a message? He knows the rules just as well as I do. If he broke the rules, that must be a sign that he wants to keep this under wraps.

Or...he's in a hurry? Yeah, if you go through the proper communication channels like runners or handmaids, you're susceptible to leaks.

I kinda wish this soldier would just spit out the message right now... But maybe he can't because Matilda's here.

Matilda, as my chief lady-in-waiting, was quite strict in these matters. She always delivered information to the top of the chain. And if my theory about Alec was right, that was something I needed to avoid.

Matilda waved to Sasha, who stopped the pianola. The *Hofballtanze* stopped playing.

Matilda's rebuke echoed clearly in the now silent practice room. "You are *not* a runner, I take it? You are before Her Royal Highness. Now, who are you? State your name and assignment. I am Matilda, chief lady-in-waiting."

The soldier saluted. "Aye, Madam Chief Lady-in-Waiting! I am a new recruit, so my assignment is yet to be determined! It will be posted after I finish my boot training! My name is Guy Peutz!"

"New recruit... Do you have proof of this?"

"Proof...my lady?" The soldier looked worried.

"Yes, proof. Don't you carry a permit?"

"Oh! Uh, yes! Of course! Always...," the soldier stammered, frantically patting himself down. "I always...hang it from my...neck?"

His complexion grew greener and greener. Then he gasped as if he'd suddenly remembered something, bowed his head, and stopped his search.

"It s-seems I've left it behind in the barracks today..."

Matilda's eyes widened.

Esfia's soldiers were handed permits to carry as identification. That was a policy my father instituted after that incident with the spy. It was a piece of leather on a string, and the soldier's name was etched into the circular part of the leather. Carrying it showed you were a proper soldier of Esfia. If you tried to sell it, you'd be sent to the dungeon without question. It was strongly encouraged for soldiers to carry it with them at all times.

"Then go fetch it now. Otherwise, I cannot recognize you as a soldier of our kingdom. I will confirm your identity with Prince Alexis as well."

Matilda was 100 percent in the right—nobody could deny that.

The soldier's behavior was now even more suspicious. The color drained from his face, having forgotten his permit—he was a swirling vortex of suspicion.

But if he went to retrieve his permit, that would mean a huge delay. Even though the barracks were in the castle, they were still quite far away, you see! Even if he sprinted the whole way, it was sure to take thirty minutes at least. Meanwhile, Matilda would go to Alec for confirmation, which would nullify the whole reason Alec asked a common soldier to deliver his message in the first place. That's what you call putting the cart before the horse.

"Wait, don't go."

"Your Highness?" Matilda looked at me dubiously.

"That man is indeed a soldier of Esfia. I recognize him."

"But, Your Highness..."

I was pretty sure Matilda believed the soldier. At most, her suspicion of him was only at 20 percent. But if there was even a fraction of doubt, she couldn't overlook it—that was her job.

"Klifford, you remember him, too, no? I know you've seen him before."

I need to increase my numbers to gain credibility for my claim. It happened yesterday, and even I remember seeing him on the training grounds, so I'm sure Klifford will, too!

Klifford looked at the soldier. When their eyes met, the soldier's previously frantic neck and limbs suddenly became petrified.

"Yes, indeed... I have seen this soldier before."

Yeah, I know!

"Thank you for jogging my memory, Your Highness."

"Glad I could help."

"He was sparring with Prince Alec in the training grounds yesterday...but in searching my memory just now, I remember seeing him elsewhere, as well."

"Elsewhere, you say?"

Is that so?

"On the battlefield," Klifford explained. "This man fought for Esfia. And after the war, he officially joined our ranks."

The corners of Klifford's mouth lifted upward. He looked intrigued.

Aha. So Klifford is a war veteran.

"My...what a strange turn of events. Guy Peutz, you say? So you've met Klifford before, then. I would love to hear more. May we speak freely?"

The soldier—Guy—was sweating profusely. "N-no, Your Highness! Know him? P-preposterous! Not at all! At best, I only maybe caught a glimpse of him from afar on the battlefield, but that's all! I may have been in battle, but all I did was run around escaping death!"

Yep. Looks like Guy remembers Klifford very clearly.

I looked at Matilda. The harsh glare in her eyes toward Guy had faded greatly. It looked like the war-buddies-with-Klifford angle worked on her. *Matilda sure thinks highly of Klifford's judgment. Maybe he won't need to go back to fetch his permit after all.*

"Matilda, now do you believe that he is a soldier of Esfia?"

"If you say he is, Your Highness, then I have no right to doubt you. But if he even so much as—"

"I know. If he causes a problem, I shall take full responsibility. So please, could you overlook it just this once?"

Matilda sighed loudly. Then she reluctantly nodded. "So be it, Your Highness. Guy Peutz, deliver your message."

"Well, um..." Guy's eyes darted to and fro. "Prince Alexis instructed that the message was for Princess Octavia's ears only."

Matilda rebuked him once again, in a way incomparable to the last. "You wish to be alone with the princess?! Not on your life, Guy Peutz!"

"But I am not permitted to deliver the message to anyone but Princess Octavia. I am under strict orders."

Uh-oh. Looks like we're heading back to square one...

I raised my hand and spoke, "In a word...you need deliver the message only to me, yes?"

So that's how it went down. We settled on turning the *Hofballtanze* on again as background noise so Guy Peutz could deliver his message in my ear while Klifford, Sasha, and Matilda stood at a slight distance.

But even that compromise wasn't reached quickly. Matilda's condition was that Guy be unarmed and undergo a body search. And since Matilda was making a big concession, there was no way I could object.

As for the aforementioned body search...I'd assumed Klifford was going to conduct it. But since Guy trembled all over and screeched, "I humbly decline!" Matilda, accompanied by Sasha, conducted the search.

I had to wait a while during the body search, so I walked over to an ornate pedestal that Matilda had brought into the practice room. My fan and Klifford's sheathed sword were sitting atop it.

That's right. I have to return this to him. Easy does it!

I picked up not my fan but his longsword, carrying it in both arms. I could carry it just fine, but it was unexpectedly heavy.

"Klifford," I called out to him. He was keeping an eye on Guy and my handmaids while watching me in silence as I walked. "Your sword. From now on, I promise that I will never take your sword away from you, no matter the circumstances."

Guy was Alec's servant, but what if he weren't? He could have been, like, a spy or an assassin. In my past life, I would have laughed it off. But I'm a princess now, sooo...

Luckily, I had yet to encounter anyone who earnestly tried to kill me. And one glance at Klifford, who'd just protected me, made me realize exactly how overly optimistic I'd been.

If the worst happened to me, even if I had my bodyguard by my side, if I took his sword away, he wouldn't be able to perform at his best. I was naive to think that it was *just a dance rehearsal*.

"There's no telling when unforeseen circumstances might arise," I said, making sure I burned it into my mind.

"I am humbled and grateful that you would return my sword to me personally, Your Highness."

Klifford ceremoniously took his sword from my extended hands and smoothly sheathed it.

Yep. My Klifford's back! Okay, now I need my fan...

But before I could reach for my fan, Klifford grabbed it first. Naturally, and without hesitation. "Your fan, Your Highness."

"Thank you... You have no reservations about touching wreven feathers, I see?" I opened my fan wide. I hadn't noticed it until I learned that other people called my fan Blackfeather, but when Matilda took it from me so I could dance, she did seem to be a little frightened of it.

With this new realization, I searched my memory...and found that Sasha had never voluntarily touched Blackfeather, either.

Touching wrevens and their feathers directly... I guess most people are creeped out by that sort of thing.

I noticed something else—at dinnertime, I always handed off my fan to the same waiter. I didn't hand my fan to him; rather, he always gestured for me to give it to him. When I'd used a white fan, I think I remembered a variety of waiters would come take it from me. But when I started using Blackfeather, it was fixed on that one waiter! *That poor waiter... I hope he didn't have such a crappy role forced on him by his peers!*

I couldn't even remember how the waiter's face looked whenever I'd handed him my fan. *Damn my piece of crap brain!*

In comparison, Klifford promised he would affix the wreven tassel on his sword hilt once I gave it to him. And it was more than that. Seeing the way he handled Blackfeather just then, it really seemed to me like he wasn't bothered at all by stories about wreven birds or by touching their feathers, either.

"Forgive me, Your Highness," Klifford said. "I also find wreven birds most favorable. That is why I have no reservations about touching their feathers."

My goodness...he is a true kindred spirit! I wish he'd said something sooner!

"Klifford, what do you like most about wreven birds?"

I love their fluffy feathers, personally!

"I like their lust for life most, I suppose. Real wrevens are far from Hell, and they do not die easily. They are also quite fertile and hale. They fly in flocks, yet they possess the strength to survive even when alone."

Now it made sense. So that was why you could see wrevens flying everywhere, even though they weren't exactly a cherished bird.

"However...wrevens are also seen as...impurity incarnate...which is why they are widely despised," Klifford added somewhat sarcastically.

"I guess our kingdom prefers to revere beautiful things that die with valor," I said.

"It would seem so, yes."

"What horseshit..." My voice was so icy that it startled me.

My face was twisted in anger from spitting out the words like a curse... So I hid it behind my fan.

Crap. That wasn't very princess-like. Not to make excuses, but a fragment of my bad memories was creeping back into my brain...and I just snapped!

Klifford, who couldn't let what I'd said slide, gave me a quizzical look. But he smoothed over it with a soft smile.

"Your Highness?"

That was Matilda's voice calling me. *What a lifesaver!*

"We've completed the inspection."

It had taken ten minutes before I finally got to hear the message, but I got it. Even though it was an unorthodox method of message delivery, it was still faster than going through the usual channels would have been.

"I see. So Father gave Alec a secret mission..."

That morning, when Alec was in the training grounds, Father had come over to him "by coincidence." Then he gave Alec some secret instructions in a way no one else around could hear.

A secret order to Second Prince Alexis as his king...

But there was more. Normally, as per Alec's schedule, he spent his mornings in the classroom. He wouldn't have been in the training grounds in the first place unless Father had done something to change his schedule.

Alec would need to suddenly leave the royal capital for a few days along with a handful of companions.

Maybe Father finally sees the value Alec has to offer... But this means I won't be able to see or talk to Alec for days?!

"However, the truth is going to be swept under the rug," Guy explained. "The official word will be that Prince Alexis is ill and must spend a few days recovering inside the castle walls. Naturally, this means he won't be able to see you for a while, Princess."

My brow furrowed. *Why does this have to happen again...?* Then again, I knew that if I heard Alec was sick, I would definitely have tried to go visit him. But in this case, Alec wouldn't be at the castle. He knew that I wouldn't be able to visit someone who wasn't home. That I would be turned away at the door if I tried to go visit him. I was okay now, since I'd gotten the message...but if I hadn't known about it, I'm sure that would have dealt a lot of emotional damage...

"Prince Alexis wishes that he could have told you personally, but he had to depart immediately, so there wasn't a moment to waste," Guy explained. "He hopes that you could at least be spared any needless worry."

"However, my knowing this goes against my father's wishes... Am I correct in assuming this?"

So that's why Alec didn't go through handmaids or the runner. Any of those people were sure to tell Father about it.

"For a new recruit and someone not even under Alec's direct jurisdiction, you sure seem to have earned his trust in such a short period of time."

How admirable! Sure, Alec may be an angel, but he's not the type of person who opens up to just anybody.

"I'm not sure I earned his trust, exactly... I just happened to be the one nearby." Guy paused, his gaze distant. "I...haven't let my surroundings influence me..."

Huh? What's going on? Guy's eyes...suddenly look like a dead fish? I've seen that look plenty on my handmaids, but this is the first time I've seen it on a soldier!

And Guy continued, the dead-fish eyes still present, "I'm sure it was a vital matter to Prince Alexis... And sadly, I'm in a small minority among the castle soldiers... And because of this, he recognized the face of even a lowly soldier such as myself."

"I recognized you, too, Guy Peutz."

"Th-thank y—"

"That reminds me, I know this may sound strange, but why did you go all green in the face when you walked into the practice room and saw Klifford?"

This is an innocent question, I swear!

"Well, that's because—" Guy stopped mid-answer and clamped a hand over his mouth.

"Yes?"

"Ah, uh, right. Your Highness...it was bloodthirst. I sensed bloodthirst coming from your bodyguard's eyes. And it's only natural that your bodyguard would find me suspicious, when I entered the practice room like that."

Something that's only detectable by a pro, eh? I mean, I didn't sense anything like that.

"You can sense those things? Quite impressive. Perhaps this was your experience on the battlefield with Klifford talking?"

"Oh, no!" Guy's voice cracked. "I know nothing, Your Highness, so there's nothing for you to worry about! I have had no association with your bodyguard, either!"

Whoa, he's gone full-on defensive. Let's slow down, buddy!

"No need to panic, dear. Lower your voice."

"Aye...forgive me, Your Highness."

"I was merely voicing my opinion, no? I meant nothing of it—you needn't worry. Forget I even said anything."

"Y-yes, Your Highness."

Oh, that's right. I almost forgot to ask him the most important question.

"Guy Peutz, is Alec still in the castle, or has he already departed?"

"I think he's still here... He's probably on his way to the castle gate right now."

So...I might be able to catch up in time to say good-bye!

16

I wasn't going to have time to change back into my everyday dress, so I put on a cloak to keep my outfit from getting dirty. Then I headed for the castle gate.

Naturally, I couldn't just announce to everyone that I was going to see Alec off. But all I had to tell Matilda was that since I was spending the day getting ready for the junior ball already, I wanted to have a little walk around the castle grounds while I was dressed up, and everything would be okay on paper!

If, on the way, I happened to feel like getting a little air, and if that resulted in me accidentally going all the way out to the castle gate, where I happened to bump into Alec...well, I was just out on a walk, you see!

Even if Father found out about it later, I'd be fine.

It was all just a big coincidence, I swear!

If I'd bumped into Alec by accident, my father could blame neither me nor Alec for it.

And I know I said I'd be meeting him by the castle gate, but it wasn't the one at the front of the castle—it was the side gate. A part of me lowkey wanted to slip out the side gate myself, but that wouldn't do, so I had Klifford and Guy accompany me. We didn't chitchat; we just walked quickly toward our destination.

Finally, I can see the side gate!

This gate was quite a bit away from the main castle gate. The front gate was so tall and wide that it made you go, *"Now that's a gate!"* It even had vicious-looking arrow slits in the cracks in case we needed to shoot somebody. Guards were posted around the clock to observe whoever came and went through the gate.

Meanwhile, the side gate was arranged so that people couldn't pass through it normally. Because of this, there wasn't a guard posted. It came with a drawbridge attached, but it was double-fortified—if you tried to lower the drawbridge to open the gate, the gate would still be closed off by an iron fence. It could only be operated from the gear chamber inside the castle. So even if you marched right up to the side gate, it wouldn't budge for you.

I wonder if using the side gate was part of his secret mission? One of the benefits of using the side gate was that hardly anyone would see you...

I strained my eyes. The drawbridge of the side gate was lowered, and the iron fence was raised halfway. There was a line of people on horseback, waiting for the fence to rise the rest of the way up.

"Alec!"

I'm not too late!

Unable to contain myself, I hitched my skirt up and ran.

Yup. This's a good dress. Even though it's fancy, I can still run in it! Thanks for choosing it, Klifford!

"Sister!"

Alec was dressed in disguise. When he saw me, he dismounted and left his spot in line to run to me.

I've gotta get in my daily Alec quota, ya know! I usually get to see him at dinner, but I guess that's not happening today... This sucks.

As for the other people who were with Alec, one of Father's bodyguards was among them. With black hair and black eyes, he was so handsome that you could tell he was swatting men away like flies when he was younger. About the same age as my father, his hair was peppered with white. He gave up his position as knight commander to be a bodyguard. But I never saw him much around the castle. *So he's the companion Father assigned? But why would he assign his own bodyguard to Alec?*

Urgh. Everyone else in the lineup besides Alec is staring daggers at me! I definitely feel unwelcome! But I can't exactly slink away with my tail between my legs now.

I snapped my fan open. Then I smiled at Alec and lied shamelessly, "My, what a coincidence! Are you going out somewhere?"

"Yes, on a long excursion. And what are *you* doing here, Sister?"

"Why, I'm out to get a breath of fresh air. Then I happened to spot you."

Operation It's All a Big Coincidence is a go!

"Prince Alexis," Father's bodyguard grumbled from atop his horse. "The gate has risen. We can pass through now."

That was knight-speak for "Move your ass." And he was right—the gate that was only halfway up when I'd approached Alec was now fully up.

Alec turned back to him. "Are you telling me I should ignore my sister?" he said defiantly. "I wish to have a little chat with her."

"Yes, but...Princess Octavia isn't—"

"Oh my. Princess Octavia isn't what, now?" I asked.

My deepest regrets, sir! I promise I won't hold Alec back! ...As much as I'd like to!

Father's bodyguard looked like he'd swallowed a worm.

"Given what Alec has said, why don't you boys get a head start?" I suggested. "After all, your prince is having an outing far from home. As his vassals, you must go ahead of him and ensure his safety."

"What a nice idea, Sister. Let's do that. Randal, you stay behind with me."

"Aye," answered one of the men on horseback in line. *Ooh! That foot soldier is the rising star Alec has had his eye on!* He already had a wife when he was a new recruit, so he was a late bloomer racing up the career ladder and was on track to become Alec's closest associate.

"The rest of you, go on ahead. I'll catch up with you later," Alec ordered in a tone so firm that it was clear the matter wasn't up for debate.

Yes... Yes, this is it! This is what I lack. That royal austerity he exudes! An overpowering aura!

Father's bodyguard narrowed his eyes. Then he looked at me. "Prince, Princess...you truly do have a close friendship."

"Why, yes, we do. Isn't that wonderful?" I smiled, shutting him out with my fan.

"I do not understand it... Prince Alexis, as you command. We shall proceed ahead of you. Please catch up with us as quickly as you can. We mustn't fall behind schedule. Now, if you'll excuse me."

Father's bodyguard bowed from up on his horse, pulled the reins, and galloped away. Then one by one, the rest of the knights followed in an orderly fashion.

Then it was just me, Alec, and Randal, who was on horseback right by the side gate. Klifford was a few yards away from me on guard, and Guy was also there.

Huh? It looks like Klifford and Guy are having a hushed conversation. And what's more...it looks like Klifford was the one who initiated? That's unlike him. I wonder what they're talking about?

In my peripheral vision, I caught a glimpse of Alec sighing gruffly as he watched the line of soldiers ride away. I returned my distracted focus back to him.

Alec looked at me directly, his green eyes blinking. "Sister. That dress...it brings out a different side of you."

"It doesn't suit me?"

"Don't be silly. I was enraptured. You look wonderful."

Okay, I'm calling it. From the natural, painless way he compliments a lady, I just know Alec is going to be a dreamboat!

"Why, thank you. It's actually for the junior ball tomorrow. I was trying it on when I received your message, so I kept it on."

"I see... I'm so sorry to bring this on you so suddenly, Sister," Alec said, his shoulders drooping. "But I knew you would come," he finished with a smile.

"And I knew you would be waiting for me, Alec."

We're brother-sister besties, after all!

There was no need to deliver an urgent message just to tell me he was leaving on a secret mission. So I theorized that this must have been his way of signaling that he wanted to see me before he left. And of course, I wasn't supposed to know that Alec was on a secret mission, so I had to come see him under the pretense of coincidence.

And that's how we wrote the thrilling tale: *Whilst on a Walk I Happened to Bump into My Brother Alec Who Was About to Leave on a Trip!*

"Peutz, I owe you my thanks as well," Alec told Guy graciously. "You did well."

"I am unworthy of your praise, Your Highness!" Guy said, cutting his conversation with Klifford short and running over to Alec.

Maybe I was just imagining things, but he almost looked relieved to be leaving Klifford's side. He did say he'd sensed bloodthirst coming from Klifford. Maybe he just didn't like Klifford, even if they went back a ways.

"But, Alec, you were way too reckless with your new recruit."

It was honestly a stroke of luck that Guy had been able to make it to the practice room in the first place. While there weren't any guards stationed at the practice room door, there were guards stationed at the doors in the hallway to get there. He had to have been stopped and questioned many times along the way.

"Well, Sister, I knew that you would understand my true intentions. Guy, did you run into any trouble?"

"Er, no, Prince..." Guy paused for a moment. "There was...no trouble. I was able to deliver the message to Princess Octavia alone."

"I am relieved to hear that. You have served me well."

"Sir!"

"Sister, about the message..." Alec cut himself off midsentence and glanced over at Klifford. I realized then that Klifford was the only person there who didn't know about Alec's secret assignment. Randal would know, since he was in Alec's party, and Guy knew, since he delivered the message to me.

And Alec knew, since he was the one Father assigned the mission to.

"Could you please send that thing away?"

By "that thing," Alec meant Klifford. Ordinarily, I'd happily do Alec's bidding without pause. But even though we'd made plans to have a private chat about Alec's dislike of Klifford...well, that chance just flew out the window, didn't it?

"Klifford, do not repeat anything you hear to another soul."

"Yes, Your Highness." Klifford bowed, his expression unchanged.

"There. Satisfied? There is no need to dismiss him."

Alec sighed heavily, his lips in a firm scowl. "I am most certainly not satisfied...but I trust you, Sister," he relented.

"Thank you, Alec." I couldn't help but reach out to pat his head.

But he gently stopped me. "Sister, please. Don't treat me like a child."

"I'm sorry... So, Alec, how long will you be away from the castle?"

"About ten days, though maybe longer, depending on the circumstances."

It seemed that this secret mission was sudden news for Alec, too. And his travel party for the mission had all been decided in advance by our father. Everything he needed was already there. And that was the very reason why a sudden mission like this was possible. But why...?

It was either a mission that only could be asked of Alec...or it was to hide Alec's absence from the rest of the castle...

Something stinks. I smell a fishy conspiracy here!

Father did entrust Alec with an important matter—that much was clear. And when you compared that with the way he'd treated Alec all his life, it should have been something to celebrate...

"I cannot tell anyone where I'm headed—not even you, Sister. Nor can I divulge any details of the mission..."

"I see..."

"But if you were to tell me you needed to know, then I—"

"I don't need to know."

Telling me about the mission in the first place definitely went against Father's wishes. It was a tiny act of defiance. But if he were to divulge the details of the mission to me on top of that, his defiance would no longer be tiny. So it would be crazy of me to make Alec tell me about his mission. Besides, there was one thing that worried me more than the mission itself...

"The only thing I wish to know is if you are in danger, Alec... Are you?"

"Dear Sister..." Alec chuckled softly. "It is you who I worry more about. I cannot protect you if I'm gone."

"It's the feeling that counts."

"Feelings are not enough..."

"Then...I ask that you return safely from your mission. I feel lonely when you're gone."

"Even when I'm gone just ten days?"

"That's right. Just ten days, you hear? No extensions."

"Understood, Sister. Shall we pinkie promise?"

"Oh...you wish to do that here?"

"Yes." Alec nodded, extending his right pinkie finger toward me.

Pinkie promise. Esfia had no such custom. It originated with me. Or rather, from my past life memories as Maki Tazawa, the Japanese girl. We would link pinkie fingers and chant, *"Cross my heart and hope to die, stick a needle in my eye"* as a sign that we'll keep the promise. Only Alec and I knew about the custom, so any third party who saw it would probably be confused. The chant was pretty morbid, too. But Alec really loved it.

I offered my pinkie finger in turn. We linked our pinkie fingers together and recited the chant.

"There. All pinkie promised." Satisfied, Alec released my pinkie finger. "I promise I will return in ten days. After all, thirteen days from now, you'll be introducing your beloved to us."

"Right..."

Bringing my fake boyfriend home to meet the family... Alec already knew about that, too?! Then there's the fact that one night has passed since Father set the date...which means I have less than two weeks!

"There's something I wish to tell you alone before then," Alec said.

"There's something you wish to tell me, too, right, Sister?"

"Yes. If not for your mission, I would have told you today. What a pity."

It almost made me wonder if Father's impeccable timing had been to interfere on purpose.

"Isn't there something you could tell me now?" I asked, knowing I couldn't exactly go into detail about the fake boyfriend and Klifford. But perhaps Alec could say something.

"There is...just one thing."

Ooh! You've got something to say?

Alec hesitated for a moment, then he said, "Sister...did you ever meet the late Duke Kihlgren?"

Kihlgren? His question was definitely not what I was expecting.

"I might have met him when I was a baby...but that's the same as not meeting him, I suppose."

Duke Kihlgren was deceased. He was Father's uncle, which made him Alec's and my great-uncle and our grandfather's little brother. Duke Rufus Kihlgren. While Rufus was his first name, he was more well-known for his official title of Kihlgren. It was a special title that only lasted one generation, and he was previously the Duke of Nightfellow.

"I heard that Duke Kihlgren...died the day I was born," Alec said.

"Yes, I heard he died of illness."

There were no fishy details about his death...I think. He was over eighty, so he probably went peacefully in his sleep. He was just old.

"Do you think I resemble Duke Kihlgren in some way?" Alec asked.

"Do you?"

There was a portrait of our grandfather hanging in the castle...but not of his little brother. If there were such a portrait, perhaps it was with House Nightfellow? And even if there wasn't a proper portrait, surely we could find a drawing or something if we looked hard enough.

"Alec...why are you asking me about this?"

"Father called me...Kihlgren...when he gave me the mission..."

Father called Alec Kihlgren? Today? Right as he sent Alec on his secret mission? But even if Alec did look like Duke Kihlgren, there's no way our father would mistake Alec for a guy who died of old age...right?

Alec shook his head. There was a smirk on his face. "I'm probably overthinking this. I always seem to get overly sensitive when it comes to Father."

"Alec..."

"I'll concentrate on carrying out my mission instead. I'm grateful that you came to send me off, Sister... I'd better be on my way."

Aw man, I don't want you to go...

"That's right... Just in case Peutz is reprimanded for this in my absence, would you see to it that he is unharmed?"

"Sure. I just need to vouch for him, yes?"

After all, he's the rising star Alec recruited! If the worst happens to him, I'm definitely busting out my princess privilege to help him!

"Yes, thank you, Sister." After a long silence, Alec broke it with, "Well...may I have a farewell kiss?"

"Why, of course." *Though as someone with Japanese muscle memory, it's always super embarrassing.*

Unlike the pinkie promise, farewell kisses were an actual Esfian custom. Regardless of the length of time you would spend apart, the people leaving and the people staying behind would kiss each other on the cheek. This was for a safe journey and a safe return.

The remaining party would kiss the departing party first on the right cheek, then the departing party would kiss the remaining party on the left cheek.

I brought my lips to Alec's right cheek. Then Alec pressed his lips to my left cheek.

"!"

For an instant, electricity seemed to spark where his lips were touching. But it wasn't winter... I leaned back a little, hoping Alec hadn't received the same shock I had, but it looked like he'd felt nothing special.

Huh?

"Sister?" *Is something wrong?* his eyes seemed to say.

Alec was about to leave on a mission. The last thing he needed was for me to say something that would worry him.

So I swallowed my worries and said, "Have a safe trip, Alec."

"See you later, Sister."

The World Through the Emissary of Ongarne's Eyes: 2

"...I require a breath of fresh air."

After giving the second prince a sendoff to his excursion, which had been presumably assigned that very day, Octavia, who had been making her way back to the castle, suddenly stopped in her tracks. She had been acting strong when Guy Peutz, the soldier who had been tasked with delivering Prince Alec's message to her, was still there. But now, perhaps due to the recent departure of her brother, there was a listlessness in her eyes.

"That's why I came out here in the first place. I wish to walk in the garden for a little while. Do you have any objections, as my bodyguard?"

Octavia's fan was pointed at one of the many gardens that could be found within the castle grounds. It was different in appearance from the front garden that had been built for the royal family's recreational use. Though it *was* pruned and kept up, it was a little garden that those who worked at the castle sometimes took short breaks in. Royals or nobles were not expected to go in there.

It wasn't the sort of spot a princess would take a liking to, either. However, over the past three days, Klifford had come to grasp that Octavia was the sort of young lady who actually possessed a fondness for things that a princess wouldn't ordinarily like. Sometimes, he even felt that her sensibilities were closer to that of a commoner—though he knew that couldn't be true.

"Are you sure that garden will suffice, Your Highness?"

"Yes. I prefer that garden."

Klifford bowed slightly. "As you wish, then, Your Highness."

"Don't tell Matilda. She'll certainly be angry with me."

"Surely she wouldn't be?"

That chief lady-in-waiting took Octavia's side more than anyone else in the castle. She wouldn't be angry.

"You're only saying that because you don't know just how terrifying Matilda can be, Klifford. Though you will know someday, I'm sure."

"Well…I'll pray that no such day comes."

"I mean it, you know?"

They arrived at the garden. White flowers were haphazardly growing everywhere.

Klifford narrowed his eyes. "*Lieche orchids…*," he murmured silently. He didn't know if Octavia had chosen to visit a garden teeming with Lieche orchids by coincidence or on purpose.

Octavia walked through the garden with a spring in her step, until she suddenly stopped in her tracks and grumbled. Her cloak had gotten caught on a branch. With a frown, she tried to remove her cloak… It was unclear whether she was wrestling with the tree or using a strange method to pull her cloak loose—either way, she was having a hard time of it.

"Oh no!" she yelped. Her cloak had torn.

"May I?" Klifford asked, extending his hand. He lifted the entangled cloak with one hand and freed it from the branch.

"Thank you," Octavia mumbled awkwardly. "You're quite handy, Klifford…," she added, looking right up at him.

"But unfortunately, you can no longer wear that cloak. Allow me to carry it for you," he said, draping Octavia's ripped cloak over his arm.

"Thank you. I shall have to be more careful when I walk, now that I don't have a cloak to rely on."

Knowing she needed to get away from the bramble to protect her dress for the next day's junior ball, Octavia treaded slowly and carefully. The red-and-black dress fluttered around her ivory-white back.

When dressed in this gown that he had chosen, there was an air about Octavia that lifted his spirits. Ordinarily, the moment someone became Sovereign to an Adjutant, the Adjutant was—in a way—controlled by his Sovereign's emotions. Klifford had assumed that he was immune to this, but—either because she was his second or because he had chosen her himself—he did seem to be affected by her to some extent. It was the same when he was her dance partner. When he saw her cheerful smile, he was captivated...

I felt charmed... It was a change of emotion that he found difficult to comprehend—even though it was his own.

"It occurs to me," Octavia said, suddenly looking up from her dress. "I never got your opinion."

"My...opinion? About what, Your Highness?"

"About the dress you chose for me. Am I doing it justice?"

It was a question that caught him completely unawares. Much like the time he asked Octavia for a command and she'd given him an unexpected answer.

She looked a bit anxious. "Answer me honestly."

On a fundamental level, Octavia was easy to read. But just when he thought she was a simple girl, she would occasionally react or talk in a way completely outside what he imagined. That's why she was hard to understand. In heart, and in mind...

"You wish me to answer...honestly, Your Highness?"

"Yes," Octavia said, solemnly nodding and bracing herself for the worst.

"Then I shall give you my honest opinion."

"And what is it?"

"I was surprised when you decided to wear that dress."

"Oh...really?" Octavia tilted her head.

"Yes."

"So you mean to say that I shouldn't have chosen this dress?"

"Not at all. I am very honored by your decision, Your Highness. It is my opinion…that no one else could wear that dress as gracefully as you."

It suits her… Those words aren't nearly strong enough.

"Oh, Klifford. You flatter me too much." Octavia blushed slightly and dropped her gaze to the ground.

"Not at all."

As he beheld his Sovereign, surrounded by the white blooms, a sudden thought hit him.

"However…it's missing something. I suppose you won't be able to adorn yourself in this way tomorrow, but…"

The white-petaled Lieche orchids bloomed proudly all about the garden. Their long, slender, and lush petals flared outward and curled. Klifford reached for a bloom and picked it.

As Klifford approached Octavia, she did not pull away. She simply stood there vulnerably. It was just as she had told him yesterday: *"It means that I trust you."*

Klifford smirked and tucked the Lieche orchid into her flowing silvery hair.

"This just might make the ensemble perfect."

Octavia stared blankly at him. Then she softly touched the orchid. "A Lieche orchid?"

Klifford nodded. Lieche orchids—their beautiful white petals were edible and medicinal, but their seeds were poisonous and could shatter the very mind of anyone who ingested them. These flowers had two sides to them. As medicine or poison, if distilled, they fetched an exorbitant price at market. Only in a castle like this could they be allowed to simply bloom beautifully.

"In Ongarne, in the farthest reaches of Hell, it is said that there is a pure land where Lieche orchids bloom. Only the Goddess of Death who rules over Hell may walk there."

Octavia's ethereal blue eyes gazed at Klifford. "Are you saying that the Lieche orchid suits me well because I carry Blackfeather?"

"Is that not to your liking?"

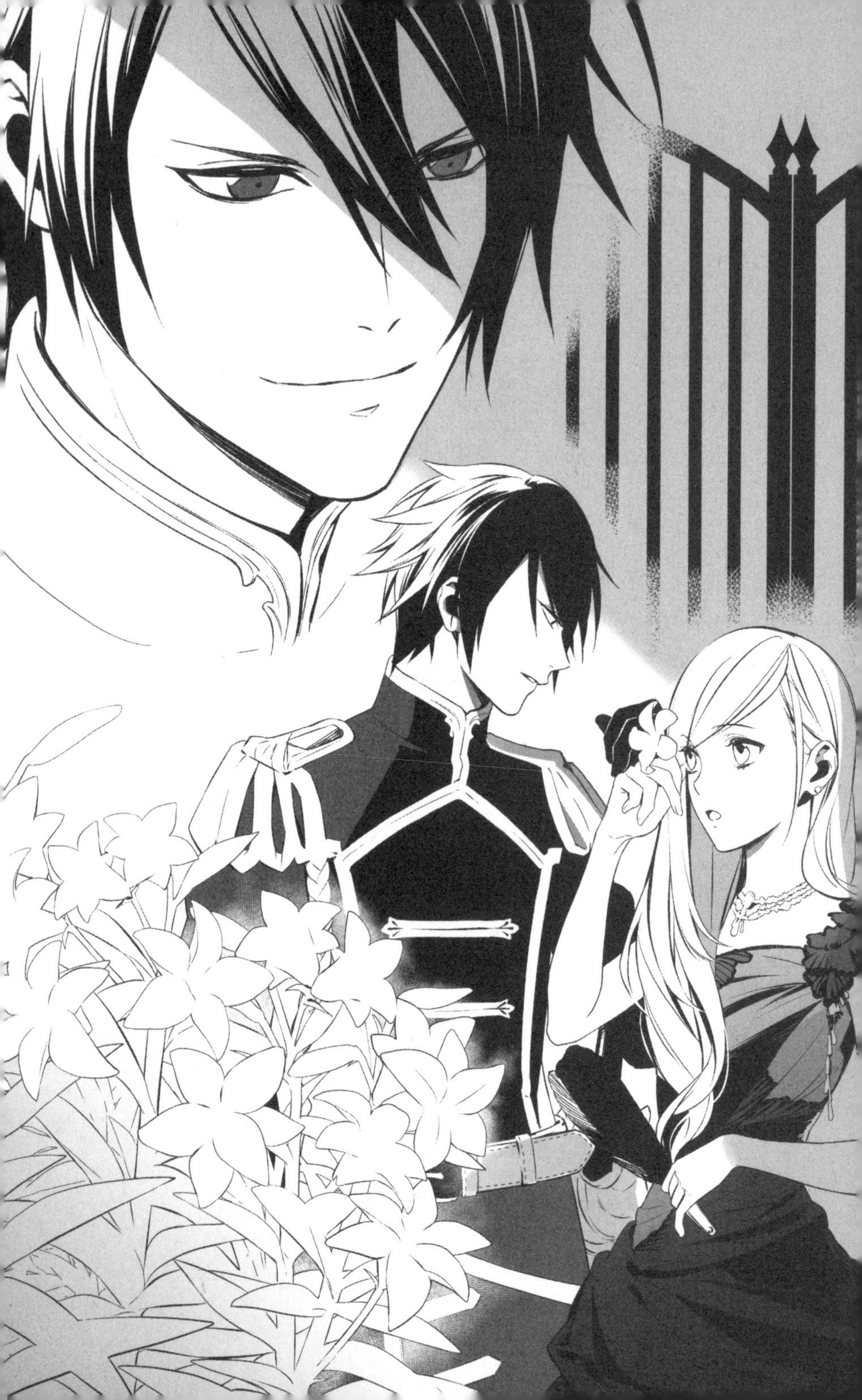

"I feel a little…conflicted. But instead of a bejeweled hairpiece, I'd rather adorn myself with something living like this flower… I do like it. So…"

The rest of her sentence was not for Klifford to hear. She whispered the words to herself. Octavia smiled, reveling in a happy memory.

But she quickly suppressed her smile and snapped Blackfeather open to expel the memory.

Octavia, who had not attended a junior ball for quite some time, exceeded Countess Rosa Reddington's expectations by accepting the sudden invitation.

And the next day, Octavia would arrive at the junior ball draped in a dress just like the Goddess of Hell…with the Emissary of Ongarne by her side. A trained eye would notice. But there's no telling how such people would react.

And thus, the wheels of fate began to turn…for those who were once basking in the pretense of peace.

—Fin.

Afterword

Hello! I'm Mamecyoro.

Thank you for reading *The Princess of Convenient Plot Devices*. I'm currently serializing this novel series on the novel publishing website *Shousetsuka ni Narou* under the same pen name. I'm so thankful that it's now been published in novel form.

I've always loved girls' novels, but I only read them. As much as I enjoyed reading them, I always thought that writing them would be too hard…so I treaded water like that for many years until I finally started writing a novel as a personal challenge to myself—and this is that novel.

The concept for this novel was born from a few ideas: Let's make it a European-style isekai fantasy with a female lead! Let's add some romance! Let's make it a comedy at heart! And let's shove my special interests into it and just write it how I like it!

I think my work speaks for itself, so instead of talking about the novel, I'm going to just talk a little about my pen name and the title and such.

I got the name *Mamecyoro* by combining the names of the two cats at my parents' house: Mame and Cyoro. I think this happened because when I had to enter my name in the *Shousetsuka ni Narou* website, I was probably thinking, *Aw man, I wanna pet my cats. I wanna just bury my face in their belly floof*…somewhere in the corner of my mind. When

I heard I was going to be published, I wondered for a minute if I should change it, but I decided to keep it! So I did.

The published title of this novel series in Japanese is: *Watashi wa Gotsuugou Shugi na Kaiketsu Tantou no Oujo de Aru*, but in *Narou*, it was *Watashi wa Gotsuugou Shugi Kaiketsu Tantou no Oujo de Aru*. So there's a subtle difference: one hás a *na* and the other doesn't. If we'd kept the title the way it was in serialization, there would be nine kanji all smashed together in a row in the middle of the title. So after bouncing a few title ideas back and forth, in the end, we settled on *na*! Just the addition of one hiragana character made the title a little softer…or at least that's what I think.

Moreover, the title feels a tad long to me when I write it out, so I call it *WataGo* for short. My PC desktop is covered with a hoard of folders titled *WataGo*.

And *WataGo*'s illustrations were drawn by Mitsuya Fuji. When I first saw the Octavia illustration, it was so on point that I actually gasped in awe.

Lastly, I would like to thank my editor for giving me the opportunity to be published and for giving me all sorts of advice on the story.

There will indeed be more! The story is still in its early stages in Volume 1, so I hope we can meet again in Volume 2.

Mamecyoro

HAVE YOU BEEN TURNED ON TO LIGHT NOVELS YET?

86—EIGHTY-SIX, VOL. 1–11

In truth, there is no such thing as a bloodless war. Beyond the fortified walls protecting the eighty-five Republic Sectors lies the "nonexistent" Eighty-Sixth Sector. The young men and women of this forsaken land are branded the Eighty-Six and, stripped of their humanity, pilot "unmanned" weapons into battle...

Manga adaptation available now!

WOLF & PARCHMENT, VOL. 1–6

The young man Col dreams of one day joining the holy clergy and departs on a journey from the bathhouse, Spice and Wolf. Winfiel Kingdom's prince has invited him to help correct the sins of the Church. But as his travels begin, Col discovers in his luggage a young girl with a wolf's ears and tail named Myuri, who stowed away for the ride!

Manga adaptation available now!

SOLO LEVELING, VOL. 1–6

E-rank hunter Jinwoo Sung has no money, no talent, and no prospects to speak of—and apparently, no luck, either! When he enters a hidden double dungeon one fateful day, he's abandoned by his party and left to die at the hands of some of the most horrific monsters he's ever encountered.

Comic adaptation available now!